AS TOLD BY THE OTHER WOMAN

Written By: Janaya Black
Copyright 2006
Cover Design By:
Ken Baker and Tyrone Staples
Edited By: Patricia Barthwell

To Rev Edwina!

Thank you!

Janaya Black

Published by:
Black-Smith Enterprises
www.black-smithenterprises.com

As Told By the Other Woman

On the cover: Jai Fears
Model, singer, actress, choreographer, and songwriter. Seen in breakout roles for major motion pictures such as *The Wood*, *The Rundown*, *MVP*, and *Crossover*. For more information on how to contact or book this artist, please visit www.aleciajai.com

Published by: Black-Smith Enterprises 4/2006

ISBN: 0-9762720-1-6

Printed in the United States of America

Acknowledgements:

Thank you, Lord, for blessing me with the gift of words. I ask that you would guide me and give me the wisdom I need to do what is right.

This book is dedicated to my grandmother, Delores J. Washington. Though she is not here with me physically, I know that she is smiling down on me. I want to say that I love you, grandma, and I miss you more than I could ever say. I hope that "your Nikki" has made you proud.

To Rockey, you complete me! I don't know where I'd be without you and I thank God for you everyday. Dre and MaKinlee, Mommy loves you!

To all of my family, friends, and reading fans, thank you for all of your support! It is truly a blessing to be able to entertain people by creating stories, which is what I love to do.

I hope that you enjoy it-

Janaya

As Told By the Other Woman

Prologue

"No!" she screamed, as she sat up in her bed, heart racing, in a cold sweat. She sat for a moment to get her bearings, as she massaged her temples trying to get the smell of gunpowder and blood out of her nostrils.

"It was only a dream…it was only a dream," she murmured over and over again until she finally started to believe it.

Going back to sleep was out of the question, so she just sat on her bed and rocked herself softly, trying to forget about the sound of the gunshot and the brain matter splattering all over the wall.

"I'm not crazy, just a bad dream…she'll be here in the morning, and then it'll be alright," she reassured herself. "She'll make them understand."

The reporter who wrote the story on Marion Hayes was coming to see her tomorrow, and she couldn't wait. There had been too many sleepless nights. She knew that once she was able to tell her story, then she too would be able to find peace. Maybe.

"She'll make them understand," she whispered, as she looked at the star filled sky through the bars on her window.

Vanessa

As I turned my car down that all too familiar stretch of road that led to the Wayne County Women's Correctional Facility, I had a strange sense of dread. It had been a little over a year since my last visit when I found out that my friend, or someone I considered a friend, Marion Hayes had committed suicide.

I had pledged to become the voice of emotionally troubled women who were imprisoned. After a lot of investigation, I found that many of the women in prison had stories that were much deeper than what would ever be told in the newspaper or shown on the news.

Many of these women had horrible childhoods, were victims of abuse, or had simply been victims of very unfortunate circumstances. After I did the story on Marion Hayes, I became determined to be a voice for women who couldn't find a voice of their own.

Today I was on my way to interview Timberlynn Crawford, a woman who was imprisoned for murdering her lover's wife. The case file said that she had shot the woman in the head in cold blood, but when I studied the woman in the picture, her eyes told a whole different story. I had seen that look before and up to this point my gut had never been wrong.

I made my way down the cold concrete hallway that led to the guard station and patiently waited for the guard to check my I.D.

"Long time no see," she said smiling.

"Yeah," I replied.

"Who you here to see this time?" She asked.

"Timberlynn Crawford," I responded as she buzzed me in.

I was left alone in the visitor's cell to wait for Ms. Crawford, so while I waited I set up my recorder and got my note pad ready. No sooner had I set my bag on the floor, then the guard was ushering in a petite young woman with handcuffs and shackles on her feet.

As she shuffled to the table, she kept her head down so that her long hair covered her face. I shifted in my seat to catch a glimpse of her features, but she kept her eyes to the ground even after the guard finished securing her restraints.

After a long moment of silence, I finally said, "Hello, Ms. Crawford, my name is Vanessa Jackson and I am here from the Women's Lib Magazine to interview you."

She slowly lifted her eyes and turned toward me. I was shocked to see that this woman appeared to be barely more than a girl. She had caramel brown skin and black hair that hung past her shoulders. Her soft brown eyes held a meekness that belied her age. Her face told me that she couldn't be more than nineteen or twenty years old.

"You can call me Timber," she whispered.

"Ok, Timber, would you like to begin with the interview?" I asked softly.

"Yes…I've been waiting a long time for this, Ms. Jackson. Thank you so much for picking me. I read the story you did on Marion Hayes and it was really nice," she said, as she fumbled with her hands.

"Thank you," I replied watching her with uncertainty, "I'm ready whenever you are."

"Ok…I just have one question before we begin," she said.

"What's that?" I asked.

"Will you make them understand?"

I looked her in the eye and said, "I'll try."

Chapter 1

Ever since I was a little girl back in Grand Rapids, all I ever wanted was for someone to love me-my mother, my father, my sister, anyone. But, it always seemed like I couldn't ever do anything right. No matter how good my grades were in school, how good I danced at my recitals, or how well I cooked dinner, nothing was ever good enough.

My parents would always make a big fuss over my sister and just pat me on the head and say, "Alright now, Timber." What they really meant was, "Get lost, Timberlynn so we can concentrate on the one we love."

I couldn't really blame them though. Skye was perfect. She was beautiful, smart, and talented. There wasn't anything she couldn't do- perfectly. She would walk into a room and all eyes would immediately focus on her. Her hazel eyes were her best feature and her long black hair was always perfectly styled. She always wore the nicest clothes and shoes. Part of me was in awe of her and the other part of me was so jealous that it made me physically sick at times.

I tried so hard to be like her, but she would just laugh at me and tell me I was silly.

"Timber, why don't you just be yourself?" she'd ask.

"Because nobody likes me," I'd say.

"Then maybe you should just disappear! Poof, be gone!" she'd say and then laugh at me when I ran to my room and cried.

She told me that so many times that by the time I was fourteen, I eventually started telling myself that I should just disappear. I began to try to fade into the background. I stopped trying to please my parents or anyone else. I even stopped bathing, I stopped combing my hair, and going to school on a regular basis. After three weeks of that, I smelled so bad that my mother forced me into the tub and scrubbed my body with a scrub brush. Then she chopped my hair off, because she felt that if I wasn't going to take care of it then I didn't need it. After that, she left me in a crying heap in the middle of the bathroom floor. My sister just stood by and shook her head silently with sadness and pity in her eyes.

That evening I went to my daddy and tried to make him understand.

"Daddy, look at me," I cried, "don't you care about me at all? Look what she did to me! Look what she did to my hair! I look like a boy!" Then I fell to his feet sobbing.

"Timberlynn, get up! You bring this stuff on yourself. What was your mother supposed to do? You haven't bathed yourself in three weeks! Do you know what an embarrassment that is to us? And what about your sister? She has to listen to the other kids snicker behind her back because her younger sister wants to be filthy for attention. Now you want someone to sit here and feel sorry for you? Timber, you've got to grow up!"

"Yes, Daddy," I said, as I picked myself up off the floor.

After that, I skated through life in a bleak existence until I was sixteen. I didn't speak unless spoken to, barely ate, and rarely left the house for anything other than school unless I was forced. Then one day I decided that I wanted to feel again, so I started cutting myself.

The cutting let me feel something other than emotional pain. It gave me a sense of being. Before long, I had to cut deeper and deeper to get a rush from it. I thought it was pretty therapeutic until my mother found me passed out on the bathroom floor from losing too much blood.

That's when the therapy started and I found out that my parents did love me a little bit. My mother cried bitterly through the sessions, as I expressed my feelings of detachment and feeling unloved. My father just stared blankly into space as my therapist told them that I had a serious problem and they would need to start paying a little more attention to me. They tried really hard to make an improvement, but old habits die hard. After six months, they were tired of trying and so was I.

Two things came out of that experience; I decided it was time for me to leave home and I started stealing. One night I took all the cash I could grab while my parents were sleeping, and then I hit the road.

Chapter 2

So there I was... on a bus headed to Detroit with three hundred and fifty dollars in my pocket. I had no idea what I was going to do when I got there, but I was sure it couldn't be worse than living in a home where nobody cared if I lived or died. So when the bus pulled into the Greyhound station, I slowly exited and stared at the people walking by.

The people here were a lot different from the people I had grown up around in Grand Rapids. They moved faster and didn't give anyone else a second glance. That was just fine by me, because I didn't want to be noticed anyway. I just wanted to find a place to lay my head and figure out what I was going to do next.

Somehow I managed to find an inexpensive motel to crash in for a few days, but from the looks of it, I didn't think I would want to be there for too long. There were hookers and crack heads all over the place. I figured with the clientele that was hanging out in the parking lot, the caretaker wasn't going to make a big deal about my age as long as I had the cash.

I walked into the front office and nervously eyed the lady behind the counter who was busy watching a small television. She was a hefty woman, with salt and pepper hair that framed her face with big roller curls, and smooth dark skin. I knew that she'd heard me come in since the bell chimed, but she still didn't turn around. So, I just stood patiently at the counter and waited. Finally, a commercial came on and she turned off the television and turned her attention to me.

"Can I help you?" she asked curtly.

"I need to rent a room for the week," I replied timidly.

"That'll be sixty-five for the week. You'll be in room 265," she said.

I slid the money over the counter, took the key, and hurried out as fast as I could. On my way to the room, I had to walk past a group of hookers, who looked at me and snickered.

"A little young to be out this late aren't ya, honey?" one of them asked. I just kept my head down and clutched my bag to my chest as I hurried by.

When I finally made it in to room 265, I stood in the dark with my back against the door breathing heavily. I tried to will my heart to slow down but it wouldn't because I was so scared. I had never been away from home before and I had never encountered people like this.

"Calm down, you big baby," I told myself, "You're on your own now. You can't show fear. No fear."

I took a deep breath and turned on the light. The room was like a throw back to the seventies with green shag carpet and plaid wallpaper. It was tacky but clean, and it would have to do for now. After I bolted the door with all the locks, I sat down on the bed deep in thought.

As I sat staring off into space, my eyes fell on my bag and before I knew it I had a gleaming new razor in my hand.

"Where did you come from?" I said to the razor as I examined it closely.

I sat there for the longest time staring at that razor, as the urge to cut myself just a little bit raged in my mind.

"No!" I told myself putting the razor back in my bag, "You will be for protection only."

With that battle out of the way, I fell exhausted on to the bed and went straight to sleep. It had been a long night and I had a big day ahead of me.

Chapter 3

I woke up the next morning and sat in bed trying to figure out what I was going to do next. I knew that I had to find a job fast because three hundred dollars wasn't going to last very long. The problem was I was only seventeen and I didn't know how to do anything. I had never had a job before and had no idea where to start. After a few more minutes of procrastination, I finally got dressed and went over to the front desk to see if maybe they were hiring.

"Excuse me," I said to the lady I checked in with the night before.

"Yeah?" she said

"Are you hiring?" I asked timidly.

The lady smiled and said, "Not at this time, honey. How old are you anyway?"

"Eighteen," I lied nervously.

"Oh," she replied eyeing me suspiciously, "eighteen, huh?"

"If you're not hiring then I'll just go…" I stammered afraid that she was on to me.

"Wait a minute! Calm down. Here, take this… it's the wanted section from the paper. There're plenty of places downtown that are hiring."

"Thank you," I said gratefully, as I took the paper. "How do I get downtown?"

"The bus stop right out front will drop you off right smack in the middle of town and you can get a good start from there," she said.

I smiled thankfully and turned to go.

"Hey…," she called out, "you be careful out there."

"I will," I promised as I walked out.

I followed her directions to downtown and began to make my way through the classified list. By late that afternoon, I had applied for five jobs and was turned down on the spot for all of them because I didn't have any experience. I couldn't understand how anyone expected me to get any experience if no one would give me a chance.

By now I was starving, so I looked around for somewhere to eat and didn't see any fast food restaurants around. A little further down Jefferson, I spotted a CVS and opted to grab a bag of chips and a pop, so that I could get back to my mission of finding a job.

As I made my way to the store, I just happened to glance to my right before crossing the street, and in the window was a sign that read "now hiring". I looked up at the building and saw that it was a Powerhouse Gym. I stood there on the curb for what seemed like forever trying to convince myself to go in there and apply for a job. Not just apply for the job but to go in there and get a job. I couldn't afford to let this one slip through my fingers because the money in my pocket would only last me another two weeks… if I was careful.

"Just go in there and talk like you have some sense!" I told myself, as I inhaled and walked through the door.

"Look straight ahead and not at the floor," I grumbled under my breath, as I marched up to the front desk with a cake-eating grin on my face. My confidence was quickly fading as I stood there waiting for the receptionist to hang up the phone. I was so nervous that I'm pretty sure I held my breath the entire time.

Smiling pleasantly, she looked up at me and asked, "Can I help you?"

"Yes, I'm here about the position you have posted in the window?"
"Ok," she replied and handed me a clipboard with an application attached to it.

"Fill this out and bring it back when you are done, ok?"

"Ok," I replied.

As I sat there staring blankly at the page in front of me I began to panic. I could feel my mouth go dry and my heart begin to hammer in my chest. What if I fill this out and they see that I don't have any experience and they send me away like everyone else did? More rejection…I couldn't stand any more rejection. I needed to relieve some of the pressure that was building up inside of me, I needed my razor so that I could let the blood flow and make it all go away. I needed this job and I couldn't leave without it!

"Calm down, Timber," I told myself, "just calm down. No cutting today...just confidence. This job is yours, all you have to do is go get it."

As I began to fill out my application, I found myself making up all kinds of interesting lies to build up my resume. I made up things based on what I had seen on TV and heard about from other people. I hoped it sounded convincing because I wasn't about to go up to that desk and ask that girl for another form.

My breathing went back to normal and I completed my application. When I was finished, I went back to the girl at the front desk and laid the clipboard on the counter.

"Thank you," she said, as she reached for my application.

"Is the manager in?" I asked.

"Yes he is," she replied pleasantly.

"Could I speak with him please?"

"Well, ma'am, I would be happy to take your application and if we are interested, someone will call you back for an interview," she said.

"If it's all the same to you, I would like to hear the manager tell me that. Thank you," I shot back with a false smile plastered to my face.

"Ok then, have a seat," she said sucking her teeth and rolling her eyes.

As I walked over to the chair to sit down, I had to inhale deeply because I realized that I had been holding my breath again. I couldn't believe that I just had a moment of boldness! I heard the girl page the manager on the loud speaker and my palms started to sweat. What was wrong with me?

Before I could start another argument with myself, a clean-shaven white man with brown hair appeared before me with an award-winning smile on his face.

"Hello, I am Dan Griffin, the general manager. How can I help you today, ma'am?" he asked politely.

I took a deep breath and said, "Sir, I am here for the position that you have posted in the window. I just wanted to meet you face to face and tell you that you can go ahead and take that sign down, because I am the only one you need to see. I am a good worker and I will always be here on time!"

"Is that so?" he smirked with a twinkle in his eye. "Do you even know what position it is that we are hiring for?"

"Sir, it doesn't matter. I need a job and I am willing to do anything," I gushed.

He stood there and looked thoughtfully at me for a moment and then said, "Step into my office."

I moved so fast that I don't even remember leaving the lobby or entering his office. The next thing I knew...I was looking at family portraits placed behind a massive oak desk with a high back chair. He looked over my application and after a long moment he laid it down on his desk and eyed me suspiciously. I immediately began to squirm in my seat.

"This is very interesting," he began, "you have five years experience as a dietician?"

"Yes," I replied nervously.

"And you graduated from Michigan State University just last year?" he asked with one eyebrow raised.

"Uh…," I laughed nervously.

"So you're twenty-one, huh?" he inquired.

"Yes, sir…I mean no sir. I'm only seventeen, but I will be eighteen real soon," I stammered.

"So why did you lie on your application?" he pressed looking me square in the eye.

"I'm sorry, but I really need this job. I've been to so many different places today and they all turned me away because I don't have any work experience and…" I babbled, as tears sprang up in my eyes.

"Stop…just stop right there. Look, I don't know what your story is but let me give you a little piece of advice… you can't lie worth shit. Your eyes are a dead give away. And another thing…," he continued, "I don't like liars…"

"I'm sorry I wasted your time, sir," I said embarrassed, as I moved toward the door.

"So…if you ever lie to me again, you'll be fired on the spot," he finished, still looking me dead in the face.

I stopped in my tracks and turned around in disbelief. I thought my ears were playing tricks on me so I asked, "Are you giving me a job?"

He smiled and said, "On one condition… you never lie to me again."

I nodded my head in agreement because there was a lump in my throat and I didn't want to sit in this stranger's office and cry like a baby.

"I am going to give you a chance, Ms. Crawford- is that your real name?"

I shook my head.

"I am going to give you a chance because you remind me of my daughter and something tells me that you need this job more than even you know. Now, I am going to start you out in janitorial full-time. Can you handle that?"

"Yes, sir," I whispered in disbelief.

"Ok, you be here tomorrow at nine 'o clock sharp. Don't disappoint me, Ms. Crawford," he said sticking his hand out for me to shake.

"I won't let you down," I promised.

That evening, as I walked back to the motel from the bus stop, I tried to remember the last time I felt this happy. In the grand scheme of things, I didn't really have much to be happy about. I mean after all I was pretty much unloved, unwanted, and almost homeless. But somehow, I was proud of myself.

This was the first thing I had ever done right by myself. Skye had never had a job, so that gave me an automatic one up on her. That thought alone was enough to make me smile to myself. I had a job.

Walking past the front office to go to my room, I saw the woman who gave me the paper sitting at the table reading a book.

I stuck my head in and said, "Thank you for the paper."

"No problem," she replied not looking up from her book.

As I started to walk away she looked up and said, "So…did you find anything?"

I smiled and replied, "Yes…I did. Start tomorrow."

"Good for you. Name's Wanda, in case you were wonderin'. You get on inside now. Don't you be hangin' outside wit them hoes. You ain't like them, so you stay clear, you hear?"

"Yes ma'am," I replied and went straight to my room.

As I sat on the bed, I starred at the phone with a sudden urge to hear my mother's voice. Before I could stop myself, the phone was in my hand and I was dialing the number. Before I could will my finger to hit the final digit, I hung up.

"They don't even know I'm gone," I told myself suddenly overwhelmed with sadness. Then I laid down and cried myself to sleep.

Chapter 4

My first day at work was nothing like I expected it to be. Well, I didn't really know what to expect but this wasn't it.

The atmosphere was very laid back and everyone was very nice to me. I wasn't used to interacting with other people a whole lot, so I really just tried to stay on task and fade into the background. Needless to say, my co-worker, Korey, wasn't going to let that happen. She was determined to hear my life story before the end of the day.

Korey was also on the janitorial staff so she was put in charge of showing me what to do. She followed me around asking all kinds of questions and interjecting little facts about herself in between showing me how machines were supposed to be cleaned. She talked so fast that I could barely keep up with her.

Finally, after about three hours of training she left me alone. I took my time alone as my first opportunity to really explore the club and see everything. As I was wiping down the equipment, I peeked around at the members who were all dressed in workout attire that appeared to be more for the benefit of other members than for working out.

The women wore tight spandex shorts and halter-tops and didn't have a hair out of place, and the men wore tight fitting shirts with shorts that accentuated their muscular physiques. It was all pretty funny. While I was washing down the machines and trying to watch the people around me, somehow I managed to get my pant leg caught in a treadmill belt.

"Ohmygosh!" I gasped, as I dropped my rag and tried to pull my pant leg out of the machine before it tore them right off of me. I pulled and pulled but it was no use. The machine kept turning and started to make a loud noise from the resistance of me pulling the other way. After a few seconds the machine began to smoke.

By this time, I was frantic and could feel myself losing the battle with the treadmill. I was horrified because my pants were going to be ripped off of me right in front of all these people!

Just when I thought I was going to have to lose the last shred of dignity I had left, the machine suddenly stopped… and that's when I saw him for the first time.

He was the most handsome man I had ever seen in my entire life. He had caramel brown skin, dark, piercing eyes, and a goatee that outlined the sexiest grin on his perfectly shaped face. I mean…I didn't have any experience with sexy but that is the only way I could have ever described his smile. He was fine and I didn't know any better. If only I could have known then what I know now, I wouldn't have given him a second glance. That man was the devil.

"Are you ok?" he asked with amusement in his eyes.

"Yes," I said quickly, as I tried to untangle myself.

"Wait a minute, you're making it worse. Let me help you," he laughed, as he unhooked the belt and dislodged my pant leg, "There you go."

"Thank you," I said under my breath, as I scrambled to my feet and hurried out of the gym.

I ran to the employee locker room as fast as my legs would carry me. I sat there and cried like a five year old. I was so embarrassed I didn't know what to do next. I couldn't go back out there! Not for anything! But, I needed this job.

"Stop being such a baby!" I told myself out loud.

"Yeah, stop being such a baby," a voice said behind me.

I jerked around to see who it was and there he was standing there just as pretty as he pleased grinning at me.

"What do you want," I snapped, as I tried to wipe away any trace that I had been crying.

"I just came to make sure that you were ok," he replied.

I just sat there glaring at him, as he continued to grin like a cat that just ate the canary.

"I'm fine, thank you. Now if you don't mind, I have to get back to work," I said abruptly, as I jumped up and started toward the door.

"Well, if you need anything...anything at all...just ask. Ok?" he said staring at me intently.

"Ok," I whispered shyly. All of a sudden my mouth went dry and I was very unsure of myself.

"By the way, my name's Tre. Try not to get stuck in anymore machines, ok?" he threw back as he walked out of the locker room.

"Yeah," I mumbled, "I'll try."

As I stood there in the wake of his presence, I tried to will my heart to start beating at a normal pace. I had never felt like this before and I wasn't really sure if I liked it. Right then I decided that it would be in my best interest to stay as far away from Tre as possible.

If only I would have listened to my own advice.

Chapter 5

"Hey there, Sugarpie," called Wanda, as I made my way to my room.

"Hi, Wanda," I called out waving.

"Come in and sit with me for a while," she said, folding up her newspaper.

I hesitated for a moment and then made my way awkwardly into the lobby and sat down.

"So how was your first day of work?" she inquired.

"Ok, I guess…I got through it ok…I guess," I stammered, as I fidgeted with my hands.

"Couldn't have been that bad, could it?" Wanda chuckled, "You'll be fine. So you gone tell me your name or what?"

"Timberlynn."

"And may I ask…Timberlynn…what you are doing here?" she asked pointedly.

I decided after my last attempt at lying that it would be better for me to just tell the truth, or stick as closely to it as possible.

"My parents put me out and so I came to Detroit to try and make a way for myself."

"Don't you have no family to take you in, girl? This ain't the place to be tryin' to get your feet wet," she chided.

"I'll be ok. This is the most alive I've felt in my whole life…" I said honestly, "at least at work, I'm needed for something."

Wanda shook her head with a look of pity on her face.

"Well you just make sure you be careful. Cause them streets ain't kind…they'll eat you alive if you ain't careful. Remember that," she warned.

I smiled and replied, "I will and thank you."

"Alright now, you get on inside," she ordered.

And with that, I went back to my room with a smile on my face. If I wasn't mistaken, I had just made my first friend.

Chapter 6

"Damn, girl! I can't believe you got stuck in the treadmill!" Korey laughed, as she slammed her locker shut. "Timberlynn, do you realize that I have been working here for over three years and I have never seen anyone get stuck in a treadmill? That's some funny shit."

"I really didn't think it was all that funny," I replied angrily. I didn't understand how she could be so insensitive.

"Hey, I'm just messin' with you, don't get your panties all in a bunch," she chirped cheerfully and smiled. When she saw that I was visibly upset, she turned serious, "I'm sorry, don't be mad, ok?"

I stood there for a minute and then shook it off, "Ok."

"I heard Tre came to your rescue," she said slyly, "He could save me any day with his fine ass. Girl, there ain't too much I wouldn't do to get that man to give me just ten minutes alone with him…"

I rolled my eyes and walked out of the locker room and went to punch in. On the way to the supply closet to get my supplies, I almost ran into Mr. Griffin coming around the corner.

"Well, hello, Timberlynn. How are you today?" he asked cheerfully.

"I'm fine Mr. Griffin, thank you."

"How was your first day on the job?" he inquired with a gleam in his eye.

I didn't answer right away because I remembered what he said to me about not lying and I wasn't sure if he was testing me or not, so I chose to play it safe.

"It was a learning experience," I said honestly, "but today will be better."

He laughed good-naturedly and patted me on my shoulder as he continued down the hallway.

With Mr. Griffin gone I was finally free to get to my daily tasks. I decided to steer clear of the treadmills and wipe down the mirrors in the aerobic classrooms.

I was finding the work relaxing, as I went about wiping down the mirrors with rhythmic even strokes taking great care not to leave streaks. I was so engrossed in what I was doing that I didn't even see Tre walk up behind me.

"Looks good," he said out of nowhere. I think I must have jumped about a mile high because he scared the crap out of me. I whipped around to face him and he had a huge grin on his face as he openly eyed me up and down. I blushed at the realization that he had been staring at my butt while I was bent over cleaning the mirrors.

"What do you want?" I asked irritated and intimidated by him at the same time. He made me very nervous and I wished that he would leave me alone so I could finish my work in peace.

"Why are you so defensive? I just want to talk to you," he stated simply. He continued to just stare at me intently, so I began to quickly gather my things so I could leave. "Now wait a minute… where you going?"

"Why are you bothering me? This is my second day at work and I just want to do my job and be left alone."

"Is that any way to treat the man that saved your life just yesterday?

"Thank you for helping me. There, I said it. Is that what you wanted to hear?" I shot out angrily.

"I don't know why you're getting so upset. You gotta learn how to lighten up and relax, girl. You're too young to be so uptight," he teased. "Come on now, don't be mean. I actually came in here to ask you to have lunch with me this afternoon."

"I don't think so, thanks anyway," I said walking past him.

"Ok," he shrugged, "maybe some other time then."

"Yeah, maybe. Excuse me, but I have to get back to work," I said and left him to stare after me.

As I walked away, the butterflies in my stomach would not stop churning. That man excited me in a way that I did not understand, so I rationalized that it was best to avoid any contact with him period. Yet, as I continued on with my day, I found myself hoping that I would run into him again, just so I could see his handsome face.

As determined as I was to avoid Tre at all cost, I was not as fortunate with Korey. She was on a serious mission to befriend me whether I wanted her to or not. At the end of the day she tracked me down and invited herself to walk to the bus stop with me.

"Hey, you wanna stop at the Coney Island and get some dinner?" she asked.

"No." I replied shortly.

"Come on! You aren't still mad about what I said earlier are you?"

"No...I'm just tired that's all. I don't have extra money to eat out anyway."

"I got you. Please come with me, I hate eating alone," she begged.

So, finally I gave in and we went to the Coney Island. No sooner had we ordered our meals and she was off to the races with twenty-one questions that I really didn't feel like answering.

"So where you from?"

"Grand Rapids."

"Really? What made you move down here?"

"Just needed a change of scenery."

"I saw you talking to Tre in the aerobics room, what's up with that?" she inquired.

"Nothing. He just wanted me to have lunch with him. I told him no though," I shrugged.

"Nothing my ass! Girl, are you crazy? That man is F-I-N-E! Do you know how many women throw themselves at him on the daily?" she exclaimed.

Suddenly I really regretted the fact that I'd agreed to have dinner with her. I looked around wondering where the waitress was with our food. Korey was really starting to get on my nerves. I wasn't used to this much interaction with another female and I really wasn't all that comfortable with it. So, I excused myself to go to the bathroom.

"Excuse me, I need to run to the ladies room," I lied.

"Ok."

I ran in to the bathroom and slowly counted to one hundred. Then I peeked out to see if our food was on the table yet and it was, so I waited a few more seconds and then went to sit back down.

"I thought you fell in or something," she said while stuffing her mouth with fries. I shook my head and started to eat my food. I was just grateful that she stopped piling me with questions long enough to eat her food.

Finally, dinner came to a blessed end, and I escaped Korey for the night when I boarded my bus back to the motel. As I rode in blissful silence, I reflected back on my encounter with Tre. I wondered what my day would have been like if I had allowed him to take me to lunch. I also wondered why he would want to be bothered with someone like me when, according to Korey, he had women tripping over themselves to get with him.

"Oh well," I thought to myself. Only time would tell.

Chapter 7

Before I knew it, several weeks had passed and I was doing pretty well on my own. Wanda was showing me how to budget my money, so that I could save up for an apartment. Just the thought of having a place to call my own made me tingle with excitement.

Wanda had turned out to be a much-needed friend and confidant to me. She was like the mother I'd always wished I had. We had long conversations most evenings about life, love, and dreams. She knew about my leaving home, my relationship with my parents, and even about me cutting myself. I told her things about myself that I hadn't even shared with my therapist and she never judged, just listened.

She told me about her failed marriage, her dysfunctional children, and her desire to get the hell away from this motel. The only reason she still held onto it was to "torture" her ex-husband, because she knew how bad he wanted it. "Cheatin' bastard," she'd call him. Apparently she had caught him with one of the prostitutes that frequented the establishment, and from what I'd heard…it wasn't very pretty.

"See, Timber, the only thing worse than a home-wreckin' hoe, is a home-wreckin' man. These women you see prancin' around here sellin' ass ain't nothin' but trash, and that's why I'm so hell bent on helpin' you get outta here. You're a sweet girl and I don't want to see that lifestyle start to appeal to you," she stated matter-of-factly. "We gone get you in your own place in no time, you'll see."

Sometimes I would go grocery shopping with her and she would show me how to get the most for my money. Wanda was the coupon queen; there wasn't anything that woman didn't have a coupon for. Then we would go back to her house and she would show me how to cook down home meals that anyone would appreciate. I learned how to cook everything from collard greens to sweet potato pies.

One evening, at the office, she came at me from left field with something totally unexpected when she said, "Sugarpie, you really should call your mama and let her know you're ok."

I looked at her with all the sadness I felt in my heart at the mere thought of my mother. Just the possibility of hearing her voice made my heart ache.

"I can't..." I whispered hoarsely.

"Look, I know how you feel about your parents, but even the worst of parents care if their kids live or die. Now my kids...them kids are some complete fuck-ups in spite of all I tried to do right by them. Even though they don't come around to see about me, not a day goes by that I don't worry about them. That just goes to say that I'm not tryin' to preach to you, but I think you should make that call...whenever you think you're ready. Ok?"

"Ok," I choked trying to swallow the lump in my throat.

"Good, now on to more pleasant matters…," she began, as she started shuffling through papers as if she were trying to find something. After a good five minutes she smiled and held up what she had been searching for. It was a credit card.

"What are you gonna do with that?" I asked.

"We are going shopping! Got my alimony check yesterday and I feel like spendin' some money. As soon as Ronnie gets here, me and you are gonna hit the mall.

"But, Wanda, I don't have any extra money to go shopping…," I whined but she waved her hand for me to shut up.

"I didn't ask you all that, now, you go on and get cleaned up and we gone have us a good time tonight," she said in her mama voice.

I smiled and said, "Ok, Wanda."

By the time I took a shower and changed clothes, Ronnie had taken over and Wanda was making her way toward the door.

That night, I had the time of my life. She spent way too much money at the mall buying any and everything she thought she might like to have, and she wasn't selfish either. She doted on me like I was her child; buying me new clothes, shoes, and matching accessories. I was so overwhelmed by her extreme display of generosity that I just kept thanking her over and over again, until I finally got on her nerves.

"Look, girl, if you thank me one more time, I know somethin'…," she muttered, as I just grinned from ear to ear.

After shopping, we went to the movies and finished out the night at Fishbone's for dinner. On the way home, I was so exhausted from laughing and walking that I fell asleep in the car.

"Timber, wake up…we're here. Come on now, Sugarpie, I gotta go home, wake on up…," she said shaking me gently.

I opened my eyes and smiled at her, "Thanks again, Wanda. I had a good time."

"You're welcome. Now, get out my car, I'll see you tomorrow."

Chapter 8

"Timberylynn, I must say that you fit right in to the club family. I had some reservations about hiring you, but I always go with my gut and it hasn't failed me yet. You're doing a great job!" Mr. Griffin boomed smiling widely at me.

"Thank you, sir," I said shyly. I had been working there for four months without any other incidents and now it was time for my review.

Mr. Griffin sat silently for a moment in deep thought and then said, "I am going to give you a fifty cent raise. How's that sound?"

I was so excited that I could barely contain myself, "Thank you! I mean...that sounds great!" Before I realized it, I had jumped up and threw my arms around him. "Ohmygosh...I'm sorry..." I said looking down in embarrassment.

He laughed good-naturedly and held me back at arms-length, "I think that's the most enthusiasm I've ever seen over a fifty-cent raise. You keep that up and I may have to promote you! You do good work, Ms. Crawford, so keep it up."

"I will," I gushed, as I hurried out of the office. On my way to the floor I ran into Tre who was coming out of the locker room.

"What's up, shorty?"

"Nothing," I replied pleasantly. He looked startled because he was not accustomed to me being friendly.

"You feel like having lunch today?" he asked.

I stood there for a moment and weighed my options. My heart was pounding and my palms were starting to sweat. I had been avoiding him for weeks and at the same time hoping to run into him alone again.

I had watched him from a distance and I was more intrigued by him than I was willing to admit to myself. He had an air about him that made you take notice when he walked into the room. His muscular physique accentuated his natural handsomeness, and his confident stride made him irresistible to every woman at that club. Me included.

The mere fact that I watched women throw themselves at this man everyday, made me feel very flattered that he was showing me so much attention. It also scared me, but my curiosity outweighed my fear.

"Ok," I agreed. It was at that moment that my fate was sealed.

We went to lunch at a little hole-in-the-wall restaurant around the corner and I could not stop my teeth from chattering I was so nervous. I hoped he didn't notice.

"Are you cold, shorty?" he asked.

"A little," I lied.

"You want me to go get my sweat shirt out of the car?" he offered, but I shook my head no. "So what made you decide to come out with me today?"

"I was hungry," I responded.

"You were hungry, huh? Is that all?" he quipped with a smirk on his face that clearly said he didn't believe that at all. "So tell me a little bit about yourself."

"There's really nothing to tell...I'm from Grand Rapids. I don't know. What do you want to know?" I shrugged.

"Tell me what you like to do, what you don't like to do, why you like to do what you do. You know that kind of stuff."

"I don't really know what I like to do," I said after a moment of thought, "I haven't really done a lot. I like working at the club...I like spending time with my friend Wanda...other than that I really never thought about it." Suddenly I wasn't nervous anymore.

"Do you like to go to the movies?" he asked.

"I guess. The last movie I went to was when I was like ten," I said sadly.

"Well, it sounds like you got a lot of living to catch up on, Shorty."

"Why do you keep calling me "Shorty"? My name is Timberlynn," I replied indignantly.

"My bad, Tim-ber-lynn," he said putting extra emphasis on my name, "Shorty is a term of endearment that I use for the ladies, I did not mean to offend you by any means." I really didn't know what to say after that so I just continued to eat.

"Would you like to go to the movies with me tomorrow, Timberlynn?"

"I don't know..." I hesitated.

"Oh come on! You gotta live a little, it's just a movie! I promise I won't bite...unless you ask me to," he said mischievously, as he stared me dead in the face. My heart was pounding so loud in my chest that I began to wonder if I was going to have a heart attack.

"Ok," I finally agreed.

"Bet, we'll go after work tomorrow. I'll pick you up at eight."

We went back to work and I don't think my feet touched the floor for the rest of the day. I was so excited; I couldn't wait to tell Wanda about my day.

When I got home, I found her in the office reading her paper. She looked up and smiled when I walked in. "Well, what's that glow on your face all about?" she asked.

"Wanda, I had the best day today! I got a raise and...I got a date! He is so cute, and all the girls at work like him and he asked me out and we're going to the movies tomorrow and..." I gushed, as I paced around the office excitedly.

"Whoa! Calm down, I could barely understand a word you just said! Now what's this about you havin' a date. Who is this guy and why is this the first time I'm hearin' about him?" she asked, with her hands on her hips.

"His name is Tre and he works with me. I've had a crush on him for a long time but tried to stay away from him, but he finally got me to go to lunch with him. We talked and then he asked if he could take me to the movies tomorrow! I don't know what to wear or anything, Wanda, I've never been on a date before!"

"Goodness, gracious, Timber, I don't know what I'm gone do with you. Tomorrow when you get home from work, we'll go through your stuff and find you something to wear. Then I'll do your face up, ok?" she said nonchalantly.

I gave her a big hug and kissed her on the cheek. "Thank you, Wanda. I don't know what I'd do without you," I said honestly, as I watched tears spring up in her eyes.

"Get on out of here now," Wanda ordered, as she tried to turn away so I couldn't see her face, "don't start getting all mushy on me. You know I don't like that shit."

Chapter 9

I don't know how I made it through the next day at work, but I did. I was so anxious that I could barely contain myself. The day went painfully slow, but the time finally came to punch out.

On the bus ride home, I wondered what it was going to be like to be on a date with Tre. I had never been on a date before so I didn't have the slightest idea of what I was supposed to say or do.

When I got to my room, I had barely closed the door before Wanda was knocking heavily on the other side. I opened the door and she barged in with an arm full of bags and boxes.

"Ok, now we only have a couple of hours to get you ready so let's get to it," she stated in her mama voice. I knew she meant business so I hurried to take a shower and left her to pick out my outfit. I wasn't worried because she knew way more about fashion than I ever would.

By the time I had finished my shower, she had my outfit laid out neatly for me and had the curling irons steaming on the dresser. She expertly curled my hair and applied a modest layer of make-up and after she was done, she sent me back into the bathroom to get dressed. After I finished, I stood and admired myself in the mirror.

The shirt I wore was a light shade of pink that hugged in all the right places, and the black pants hugged my hips perfectly. I was really amazed at the woman staring back at me. I didn't know her, but I had a feeling that I was going to like her. She appeared more grown-up and confident than I ever was, and I was immediately envious of her.

"Did you fall in? Come on out here and let me see!" Wanda yelled.

I walked out and stood nervously by the door. "Do I look ok?" I asked.

"Oh, Sugarpie," she gasped, as she hugged me, "you look beautiful. Now you go out and you have a good time. Here's my cell phone so if things get to movin' too fast for you, then you call me and I'll come get you, ok?"

"Ok."

As she continued to fuss over my hair, there was a knock at the door.

"Well, that's him," I said nervously.

"I know. You just relax and let me answer the door…you don't want to seem too anxious. Sit down," she ordered and I immediately complied.

She opened the door and there he stood looking just as fine as ever in a fall leather jacket and turtleneck.

"Hello, I'm Tre and I'm here to pick up Timberlynn," he said with a smooth deep voice.

"Well hello, Tre, she's not quite ready yet, so would you mind waiting out here for just a moment longer?" And before he could respond, she slammed the door in his face.

I looked at her like she was crazy. "What'd you do that for?" I asked.

"Girl, you gotta a lot to learn about men. You can't make it seem like you been sittin' here waiting for him. You gotta make him wait! Besides we gotta make sure you got all your goodies in your purse."

"Goodies?" I asked with a confused look on my face.

"Yes! Like do you have enough change for an emergency phone call, lipstick for touch ups, money in case he skips out on the bill, and your pepper spray for if he starts getting too fresh," she rambled, as she rifled through her purse trying to find what she thought I should have. Finally after about ten minutes, I was allowed to open the door.

"Man, Shor…I mean Timberlynn, you look beautiful," he said looking me up from head to toe.

I blushed and mumbled a "thank you" under my breath and then grabbed his hand. I wanted to get out of there before Wanda could think of something else that would hold us up.

First, we went to the movies and then he took me to Mario's for dinner. Mario's was a very chic and expensive Italian restaurant. I felt extremely intimidated by the menu, so I just sat there staring at it as I tried to figure out what to order.

"Do you see anything you like?" Tre asked in an amused tone.

Not wanting to appear totally naïve and uncultured I said, "Not yet."

"You have no idea what to get do you?" he teased and I could feel my cheeks burning with embarrassment, so I just shook my head no. He laughed good-naturedly, as the waiter approached with our drinks and stood expectantly waiting to take our orders. "I'll have the lamb chops, medium-well, with a side salad, with house dressing and the lady will have the same."

"Very good, sir," said the waiter and trotted off.

"Thank you," I said shyly.

"Are you having a good time?" Tre asked, with a mischievous grin on his face.

"Yes, I am."

"So tell me, Timber…is it ok if I call you that?" He paused and waited for my approval before he continued, "Are you still nervous?"

"No," I said honestly, "I really want to know why I'm here with you. I mean…I see how all those girls are at the gym and I don't understand why you would want to be here with…me."

He just chuckled to himself and stared intensely at me and said, "I promise you that I will answer that question later. But right now, I would like for you to tell me who you are."

"I don't know what you mean."

"Ok. I mean who are you. Look at you! You have morphed in a matter of twenty-four hours from a shy young girl into a beautiful young woman. I mean… I knew that you were a cutie, but damn!

When I picked you up today, you shocked the hell out of me, and it wasn't just your clothes either. You had a look in your eye that almost made me think you were a whole different person…an adventurous person. And that is the girl that I want to bring out," he replied.

I didn't really know how to respond to that so I didn't say anything. I was saved from having to reply because the waiter had returned with our salads. The rest of the dinner went very smoothly and all too soon, he was driving me back home. When we got back to the motel, he walked me to my door and I stood there awkwardly not knowing what to do next.

"How long have you been staying here?" he asked.

"About four months. Wanda is helping me save up for an apartment, so I should be able to move in a few more months."

"Good. How old are you, really? And don't lie," he warned walking closer to me.

"Seventeen, but I'll be eighteen in two weeks on the twenty-third," I answered nervously backing away from him.

"Eighteen is good. I like that," he said, still walking closer, "Now do you want me to answer the question you asked me earlier about why I chose to go out with you?"

"Yes," I said breathlessly, as my back hit the wall.

"I asked you to lunch, the movies, and dinner because I want you," he said simply, as he positioned himself so that our faces were only inches apart, "I've wanted you since the first day I saw you caught up in that treadmill. I told myself that I would not rest until I made you mine. Do you want to be mine, Timberlynn?"

I nodded my head in agreement, as he put his forehead closer so that his lips were only inches away from mine. I was so mesmerized by him that I couldn't take my eyes away from his. Just the fact that he was touching me set my whole body on fire in a way that I had never felt before.

"Good. I was hoping that you'd say yes. So I'll see you tomorrow, ok?"

"Ok," I said weakly.

He kissed me softly on my lips and then took the key from my hand and opened the door. He ushered me into my room, placed the key in my hand, and then said, "Goodnight," as he walked out and shut the door behind him.

I don't even remember him leaving. I just remembered that all of a sudden I was alone in my room with the tingle of his kiss still lingering on my lips. I turned around slowly and looked at myself in the mirror.

It was the same girl I'd admired earlier in the bathroom that was looking back at me. I walked closer to the mirror and smiled. I hoped that she was here to stay.

Chapter 10

My eighteenth birthday had finally arrived, I thought to myself, as I lay in my bed staring at the ceiling. The last couple of weeks had been a roller coaster of events for me. Tre and I had been out almost every night since our first date, and I found myself falling harder for him everyday.

He took me on long walks in the park, trips to museums, dinner at fancy restaurants, and even to a gospel play. Our time together continued to be a new experience for me, because he was always teaching me something new about the adult world.

I never realized how naïve I was until he started pointing things out to me. Tre was the type of man who liked to take charge of every situation; every time we went somewhere he would order for me, decide what movie we went to, or whatever the case may have been. I didn't mind because it made me feel secure to have him take care of me. No one had ever cared before.

At work, he was business as usual and insisted that we keep a professional relationship, so that everyone wouldn't be in our business. But I couldn't help but get jealous when I saw him training with the other women in the club. I mean, I knew it was his job as a trainer but he was a big flirt by nature.

I also thought that he would over do it some days just to push my buttons. When I would confront him about it he would laugh, kiss me playfully, and ask, "Are you jealous?" But I would never give him the satisfaction of admitting it.

I wondered, as I finally got up to get in the shower, what my big birthday surprise would be tonight. Mr. Griffin had given me the day off and Wanda and I planned to spend the afternoon together, then later that night Tre promised that he would make this the best night of my life. My whole body tingled with anticipation.

After I got dressed, Wanda picked me up and took me to breakfast at the IHOP. She had the waiter bring my pancakes with a candle in the middle, and then the whole wait staff sang happy birthday to me. I could have died I was so embarrassed, but it made me feel special all the same.

Then we went shopping and she dragged me from store to store showering me with all kinds of clothes, purses, and shoes. I was breathless by one o'clock and had to beg her to let me take a break.

"Wanda, I need to sit down!" I gasped, as I sat down and tried to rest my aching feet. "You've been running around here for four hours straight!"

"Ok, Sugarpie, let's go to the café and have some lunch," she relented. So we hauled all of our bags over to a small café that was nestled inside the mall. After we settled in and ordered, she smiled at me and asked, "So, how does it feel to be officially grown?"

I sat in deep thought for a moment and then replied, "It feels good. I can't remember ever being this happy and I owe it all to you. You have only known me for a little while and yet you have embraced me like a daughter. You just don't know what that means to me. I love you, Wanda."

"Oh...," she choked, as she gave my hand an affectionate squeeze. "Honey, I thank you for saying that. You are like a daughter to me. My daughter... well, never mind that, but thank you and I love you too. But, I can't take all the credit for you feelin' so good...you been spendin' a lot of time with Tre. I'm sure that has somethin' to do with it."

"Maybe," I said trying to hide a smile by sipping my drink.

"Maybe, my ass," she chuckled. "So you gone tell me about this new thing or what. I ain't hardly seen you in two weeks!"

"Wanda...I think I'm in love. I know I am. There's no other way to explain how I feel. I mean... when I'm away from him for even a minute I miss him. When I know he's coming to get me or I'm going to see him, I get butterflies in my stomach, and when we're together my heart races. And he teaches me the most amazing things!" I gushed excitedly.

She just sat and looked at me with a wistful gaze on her face like she was reminiscing about something from her past. "I know what you mean," she said smiling to herself. "Now have you had sex with this man yet?"

"Wanda!"

"Don't 'Wanda' me, girl! It's a legitimate question."

"No," I whispered hoping she would follow suit because I really didn't want to have the whole restaurant hear our conversation.

"Well, you just make sure that when you do, and I know you will, that he straps his jimmy hat on real tight. You don't want no babies running around complicating your life. You mind what I say, hear?"

"Yes, Wanda," I agreed hoping that she would drop the subject. I made a mental note to myself not to ever have those types of conversations with her in public again.

The rest of our day was very pleasant and soon it was time for my date, so she dropped me off at home so I could get ready.

My outfit for the night was selected with tremendous care because I knew that it was going to be special. I had chosen to wear a black evening dress that Wanda had purchased for me earlier that day. It had a jeweled strap that tied around the neck and silky material that hugged down to the waist and then flowed freely and ended just above the knee.

I completed the look with some simple gold earrings and black heels. I let my hair flow freely down my back and added a dab of lipstick to top it off. Looking at myself in the mirror, I had to admit that I had grown up a lot since I had left home.

"Looking good," I told myself, as I admired my reflection. It was amazing what a little bit of confidence could do.

Then there was that much anticipated knock at my door. I threw the door open excitedly and stood back to let Tre get a good look at me.

"So, how do I look?" I asked shyly.

"You look like the most beautiful woman I have ever seen… and I mean that," he said nodding with approval, "Come on, birthday girl, your chariot awaits."

I squealed as I took his extended hand and allowed him to lead me to his car, where he opened the door and bowed as I got in. "Thank you," I giggled.

From there, we went to a restaurant called Seldom Blues, where the atmosphere was breathtaking. I had never had food so rich in my life. Tre just looked amused as I tried the different entrees he ordered. After dinner, we danced the night away while the jazz band played on and on for what seemed like an eternity.

At the end of the last song, he put his lips to my ear and whispered, "Will you stay with me tonight?"

I lifted my head from his shoulder and looked him straight in his eyes and said, "Yes."

We left and he drove to an apartment building on the riverfront. We got out and he led me by the hand to the elevator, which took us to the twentieth floor. Once we got inside, he turned on the light and I gasped. The place was beautiful. It was masterfully decorated in contemporary décor with a black and silver color scheme. It was the perfect bachelor pad.

"You like?"

"Oh, yes," I said in awe, "You can afford all this just from working at the gym?"

He laughed and said, "You'd be surprised at how much a good salesman can make. Besides, I don't live here alone I have a roommate but he is out of town on business. Now come on so I can show you around."

Tre took me by the hand and led me from room to room showing me the different pictures and art collections that adorned the walls. Then he stopped in front of the last door, which was closed.

"What's in there?" I asked timidly.

He grabbed me by the chin and kissed me softly and whispered, "You'll see. Before I open this door, I want to make sure that you understand what tonight is all about. Do you love me?"

I looked deep into his eyes and shook my head yes.

"Tonight is the night that I want to officially make you a woman…my woman; only if you want me to. If you say you're not ready, then it's ok, we don't have to go any further, but if you say yes then I'll open the door and we'll take it to the next level. So, tell me, Timberlynn…are you ready for what's on the other side of this door?"

I looked at the door for a long moment and then made my decision. Letting go of his hand, I slowly opened the door and gasped at what I saw inside.

In the center of the room, there was a massive black oak sleigh bed decorated in red and black. He had chosen black contemporary furniture to fill the room and accentuated everything with coordinating black and red accessories. To top it all off, there were red and black votive candles casting a soft light all over the room. As I looked around in awe, he slid his arms around my waist and nuzzled my neck.

"Do you like it?"

"It's beautiful, Tre."

"It's all for you, baby. Tonight is all about me and you. After this, there is no turning back. You belong to me, understand?" he whispered softly in my ear.

I turned around and slid my arms around his neck and kissed him deeply. I wanted to show him that I was ready, and willing to do whatever he asked me to do to prove my total and utter devotion to him.

As our kisses deepened, he picked me up and carried me to the bed. He laid me down and slowly removed my clothes and then his own. He then proceeded to make love to me with the utmost care and sensitivity. After he kissed every inch of my body, he entered the part of me that would belong to him forever. As he glided gently back and forth, I gasped from the pain while he kissed me softly and asked, "Are you ok?"

"Yes," I sighed, as tears ran down my cheeks.

After it was over, I lay in his arms and stared at his sleeping face. He was so beautiful and peaceful in his sleep, that I could not resist kissing his lips. Then I lay back down and fell asleep. It had been the perfect end to the perfect night.

Chapter 11

The next day, I went to work and was greeted by Korey's incessant chatter as soon as I got into the locker room. I didn't register a word she said until I heard her mention Tre's name.

"What did you say?" I asked exasperated.

"I said that Tre is a trip! He's out there parading his wife around the club knowing he got all them women pissed off! You know how he's always flirtin' with all them girls, I know they are hot!" she laughed. "I didn't even know he was married! Woo, it's going to be an interesting day today!" she slammed her locker and walked out laughing to herself.

All of a sudden, I felt sick to my stomach. I had to sit down to keep myself from falling on the floor because my legs were shaking so bad. Tears sprang to my eyes as I sat there trying to figure out how to process what I had just heard.

"That can't be right," I told myself, "he was just with me last night. Korey is wrong… all I have to do is go talk to Tre and he will set everything straight. As a matter of fact, we'll get this straight right now!"

I stormed out of the locker room and went straight to Tre's office and stopped outside his closed door. I stood there for a minute to see if I could hear anything and heard nothing, so I knocked.

"Come in," he called.

"Tre…" I began, as I walked into his office and stopped dead in my tracks. There he was sitting before me with some woman on his lap. The girl was clearly embarrassed as she giggled and hurried to get up. I couldn't say a word, as I stood there with my mouth wide open.

"I'm sorry," she said smiling, "we just got a little carried away…we've been apart for the last couple of weeks because I've been out of town…"

Tre looked at me with a smirk on his face and said, "Timberlynn, I would like for you to meet my wife, Brooke."

"Pleasure to meet you, Timberlynn," Brooke said, as she walked over to me with her hand held out. I couldn't move. All I could do was stare blankly at her hand and try to hold back the lump in my throat.

She was gorgeous. Her hair was cropped short and her skin was caramel colored, and her face had soft delicate features. She looked like a model dressed in a waist length leather coat, jeans, and high-healed leather boots.

I looked back at Tre and tried to find some sort of sign in his face to say that this was some type of sick joke, but there was nothing. His eyes were hooded and his face showed pure amusement, as if he was daring me to say something.

Brooke continued to stand before me with her hand out expectantly, so I swallowed the lump in my throat and shook her hand. "Nice to meet you too," I choked with a forced smile.

"Did you need something?" Tre asked smugly.

"I just needed to let you know that your eleven o'clock appointment cancelled," I replied still searching for some type of explanation in his face.

"Ok, thanks," he said simply.

"I'll go now," I mumbled, as I backed out and shut the door. As I walked away, I could hear their muffled voices behind the door, and the sound just drove the stake deeper and deeper into my heart.

The rest of the day was pretty much a wash because I couldn't concentrate on anything. Even though it went by painfully slow it finally came to an end. When I got home I did not stop in and talk to Wanda, instead I went straight to my room and cried my eyes out. It felt like my heart was shattered into a million pieces. I was hurt and I was angry. I wanted to hurt him like he'd hurt me and at the same time I wanted him to hold me and tell me that it was all a horrible mistake.

There was a soft knock at the door and I ignored it. After a few moments I heard Wanda's voice on the other side, "Sugarpie, are you alright? I got worried when you didn't come by."

I didn't respond and after a few minutes I heard her key in my door. She walked in and saw me curled up in a ball on my bed staring at her with bloodshot eyes.

"Oh my goodness, Timberlynn, what's wrong with you? What happened?" she asked, rushing over to hug me. No words came, just a fresh batch of tears, as she rocked me back and forth.

"Oh, honey, please tell me what's wrong."

"He's...he's married," I choked, "his wife was at the club... I can't believe he lied to me." By now I was crying hysterically, gasping, and heaving.

"Calm down, now," Wanda said softly as she stroked my hair, "Now you listen to me...you pull yourself together. Don't you let no man break you down like this, do you hear me? Look at me... now you didn't do anything wrong. He misled you and now you have to move on. You can't be carrying on with no married man. It's good that you found out early. Come on now, I'll start you a hot shower that'll make you feel better."

She set about getting my shower ready and came out to help me get undressed, then ushered me into the bathroom. In the shower, I just stood and stared at the wall as I allowed the steaming hot water to beat down on my body. Slowly but surely the hot water began to relax me and after I was done, I put on my pajamas and crawled into bed. Wanda tucked me in like I was a five-year-old and then sat on the edge of the bed and stroked my hair. As she sat, there was nothing but pity in her eyes.

"Sugarpie, I know that you are hurting right now, but you will get over it in time. The first heartbreak is always the hardest because it is your first. I wish I could say that it gets easier but it doesn't. It's just something you learn how to deal with a little better each time. It's just an unpleasant part of life. That bastard deserves to have his balls beat in with a baseball bat, but the Lord will see to him. You better believe that," she assured me.

There was a slight tinge in my heart when she said those words. It struck a chord that I wouldn't understand until much later. All I can say when I look back on it now is that karma's a bitch.

Chapter 12

I called off sick the next day because I could not bear to go back there and face him. I knew that I was being childish and cowardly, but I needed at least a day to get myself together.

Wanda came to check on me, and then informed me that she had some errands to run. She promised that she would be back later that afternoon to check on me. I could call her cell if I needed anything.

After she left, I just laid in bed for the next couple of hours until I heard a knock at the door. At first I ignored it and hoped that whoever it was would just go away, but they persisted, so finally I got up and threw the door open with irritation.

There stood Tre with a smug little grin on his face. "Why weren't you at work today?" he asked innocently. I just looked at him like he had completely lost his mind.

"What are you doing here? You know what…it doesn't even matter, just go away and leave me alone," I snapped and tried to slam the door in his face but he stopped it with his hand, forced it open, and stepped inside.

"Look, Timber, you really need to chill out. What you saw yesterday wasn't what it looked like," he explained.

"Fuck you, Tre! What kind of idiot do you think I am? I may be young but I wasn't born yesterday. What part of you being married did I miss?" I yelled.

Unfazed by my anger, he just stood there shaking his head, like I was the one that was out of order.

"If you would just listen to me for minute I could explain everything to you. Do you think I would have gone through all the trouble to be with you these last few weeks if I didn't care about you? The least you can do is let me explain," he reasoned.

"Fine," I said, sitting on the bed with my arms crossed, "this should be good."

"Brooke and I are separated right now. I filed for divorce but she's fighting it and doing everything she can to make things like they used to be. I moved out about six months ago and I've been staying with a friend of mine ever since."

"She's a model and just got back from Tokyo. Now that she's home, she fell right back in to where she left off- trying to save our marriage. But it can't be saved because I'm in love with someone else. I'm in love with you," he said, as he knelt down in front of me and grabbed both of my hands.

"Timberlynn, I'm sorry you had to find out about her that way but I really didn't know how to just come out and tell you. I was afraid that you would run from me and I can't have that. Not now, not ever. Just like I said the other night, there is no turning back...you belong to me now."

I was speechless. I was so relieved to hear him say those words that I almost broke out into a fresh batch of tears, but I retained my composure.

He loved me, I mean he had to in order to come over here and explain. Right? I knew that there had to be a logical explanation because he wouldn't just say all those things to me if he didn't mean it. Would he? My mind wouldn't let me even entertain that thought. As far as I was concerned, all was right with the world again. He wanted a divorce, so that made it all right for us to be together.

"Do you still love her?" I asked.

"Of course I do. I would be lying to you if I said that I didn't, but I am not in love with her. There's a difference. So, do you forgive me?" he asked, as he kissed me softly.

Tears welled up in my eyes as I shook my head. "Great," he murmured, as his kisses grew deeper and he started to undress me. We made love again and this time there was no pain, just pure heated bliss.

After it was over, I promised myself that I would do whatever it took to keep my man happy, so that he would never think about leaving me. I had finally found love and was not about to let it go without a fight, I thought, as I drifted off to sleep.

I was awakened by a sharp knock at the door. I knew it was Wanda and if I didn't answer, she would just use her key to let herself in.

Frantically, I threw my clothes on and tried to figure out how to handle the situation because I knew that if she saw Tre, then all hell was going to break loose. So I ran to the door and opened it just enough for my body to fit into the opening.

"Hi, Wanda," I said trying not to sound nervous.

"Hey, Sugarpie, you doing alright?" she asked.

"I feel much better, thank you. I'm just exhausted that's all. All that crying took a lot out of me," I replied yawning.

"Well do you need anything?"

"No, I just wanna go back to sleep."

"Ok, baby, you call me if you need me, ok? Tomorrow we gone start apartment hunting, so you go on back to sleep and I'll see you tomorrow," she said, as she started off to the office. I waved and closed the door with a sigh of relief.

"That was close," I sighed, as I climbed back into bed. I felt terrible about lying to Wanda but I didn't need any more drama.

"Besides," I told myself, "I'm grown and I don't have to run everything by her."

That may have been true but I still felt bad just the same. Snuggling closer to Tre, I was sure that I would get over it soon.

Chapter 13

"I'm sorry, Ms. Jackson, but visiting hours are over," the guard said apologetically.

"Ok," I said hitting stop on my tape recorder, "Timber, I'll be back on Wednesday and we'll finish up then, ok." She shook her head sadly as the guards undid her restraints and led her back to her cell.

Back at my office, I studied the case file again and focused in on the court testimony of Tre Stevens. His testimony was disgustingly one-sided.

He made it seem as though he was completely unaware of Timerlynn's affections for him and that he had not encouraged it in any way.

"I was completely and utterly devoted to my wife, I never gave Ms. Crawford any indication that there was a chance for us to be together. That woman is delusional and needs professional help," were his exact words.

"Bullshit," I cursed under my breath. The girl had issues, sure, but she wasn't lying about their involvement; I could tell. My gut was never wrong.

"How's it coming?" asked Yolanda, my editor.

"It's going," I replied. "This girl is no murderer. I can't wait to get to the meat of this one. Should be interesting."

"Well, hurry up and get it in the bag. You know I hate stories that drag. Make it happen,

Jackson!" she quipped, as she sauntered down the hallway.

Since I had taken on the prison angle, my perspective with regard to convicts and their actions had changed dramatically. It was no longer black and white because there were so many different shades of gray. I mean, don't get me wrong...right is right and wrong is wrong. If you do wrong then there should definitely be consequences. But...some cases do deserve a little more digging into.

For example, Marion Hayes had murdered her husband, but before I did her story no one knew what kind of life she had lived. That woman endured tragedy after tragedy and finally one day, her whole world collapsed. You just never knew what a person had been through until you walked a mile in their shoes. Timberlynn Crawford had a story to tell and no matter what, I was going to make sure that her story was heard.

For the rest of the week, I mentally prepared myself for my next meeting with Timberlynn. Somehow I knew that it was going to be an emotional one. Wednesday finally rolled around and once again I was sitting in the visitor's room waiting for my interviewee to arrive.

After a fifteen-minute wait, she was escorted into the room and shackled to the floor. I paid close attention to the guard and noticed that he took extra care not to pull them too harshly, as he secured all of the locks. As he took his position at the door, he searched her face to make sure that she was as comfortable as she could be. Somehow that little exchange gave me comfort, like maybe she had a protector in this god-forsaken place.

"Good morning, Timber, how are you?" I asked softly.

"I'm fine, Ms. Jackson. Thank you for asking," she replied shyly.

"Shall we begin?"

"I'd like that…," she said looking at me with glassy eyes, "I want to finish it all today. I can't go back to that cell until I tell you everything, then maybe God will forgive me. I can't sleep at night because I have horrible nightmares. I relive that day every night and it's killing me. I'm not a bad person, Ms. Jackson, I never meant to hurt anyone. Please help me make them understand… please."

I choked back the lump that was forming in my throat and hit record on my tape recorder.

"Whenever you're ready."

Chapter 14

After our little make up rendezvous, I was able to pull myself back together. Tre swore his unconditional love to me and promised that all the unpleasantness with his soon-to-be ex-wife, would be over soon enough. I still was not thrilled about the thought of being with a married man, but let's face it…he had turned me out.

We would take off in the middle of the day to meet up for sex. It was like I couldn't get enough of him and he knew it. I stopped caring about being discreet at work because I was sick and tired of all the flirting he did with the other women at the club. I became very bold and outspoken because I felt that sharing him with one woman was bad enough, I wasn't about to deal with that mess at the club too.

My attitude really pissed him off, so I had to keep my dealings on the sly. One day, Korey felt the brunt of my wrath when she made the mistake of making one of her careless comments in front of me.

Tre walked by with one of his clients, and he was wearing one of his tight muscle shirts and Korey said, "Damn, what I wouldn't do to get a piece of that! I swear I would throw it on his ass!"

I really don't know where it came from but all of a sudden I could feel my face burning and before I could stop myself I replied, "Bitch, you need to learn when to shut your fucking mouth!"

Korey just looked at me like I had lost my mind. Her mouth opened as if she was going to respond but then thought better of it. Instead she simply said, "My bad. I didn't know you had that on lock, baby girl."

"Yeah, I do," I shot back angrily and stormed out of the room. I didn't know where this newfound aggression was coming from, and to be honest, it scared me a little. Later that day I found Korey and apologized.

"It's cool...," she said waving it off, "just forget about it, ok?"

"Ok," I replied. Unsure of what to say next, I just turned and walked away.

For the rest of the day, I tried to stay focused and on task but I just couldn't do it. I found myself stopping in the middle of tasks to go find Tre just to see what he was doing. Finally, the end of the day came and I was able to punch out.

As I was putting my time card away, I felt his strong arms slither around my waist and his lips nuzzled my ear. "Where you going?" he whispered, as I closed my eyes and smiled.

"Wherever you want to take me," I responded.

"That's what I like to hear," he said, as he took my hand and led me outside.

We went back to his apartment and had our fill of each other before he dropped me off at home. As I was walking back to my room, Wanda stuck her head out of the office and waved for me to come inside.

"Shoot," I swore under my breath, as I made my way over to see what she wanted.

I plastered a big smile on my face and said, "Hey, Wanda," in my most cheerful voice.

"Is that all you got to say to me? I thought we were supposed to go apartment shopping today after you got off work? I have been sitting here for over an hour waiting for you to come home and then I see you pull up with that cheatin' rat bastard? And all you got to say to me is 'Hey, Wanda?'" she quizzed with her arms crossed.

My hands shot to my mouth in complete shock because I had totally forgotten about our date.

"I am so sorry, Wanda. I completely forgot about that," I said apologetically.

"Um huh…," she said shaking her head knowingly, "I bet you did forget. Sugarpie, what are you doing? You know that man is married and you still messin with him?"

"Wanda, you don't understand…" I tried to explain.

"Ain't nothing to understand, baby. You can't tell me nothing I ain't already heard before. Let me guess, he told you that he's getting a divorce or that he's leaving her. Right?" she spat and I just stared at the ground.

"Timberlynn, I have heard it all before. That's what that no good ex of mine probably told them hoes he was messing around with. The fact still remains that he is married and you are headed for trouble. Please take my word for it and leave him alone before it's too late!"

My head was starting to pound and I could feel my blood starting to boil. I loved Wanda, but she had no idea what she was talking about. Maybe she'd gotten burned before, but this was different and I was not about to stand there and let her make me feel bad. He said that he didn't want her and that was enough for me. I looked at her and chose my words carefully before responding.

"Wanda, I love Tre and nothing you say is going to change that. I love you and I appreciate everything that you have done for me, but if you want us to continue to be friends then you need to stay out of this," I said looking her straight in the eye.

There must have been something in my eyes that told her to let it go because she just threw her hands up and said, "Ok."

I was glad that was over as I breathed a sigh of relief because I did not want to argue with Wanda. She was the only friend I had and I didn't want to lose her.

"So, can we go apartment hunting tomorrow?" I asked hopefully.

"I don't think so, I'm pretty sure I'll be busy tomorrow," she said curtly.

"Oh…ok, then," I said sadly, as I turned and walked out. I couldn't believe that she was still mad at me. I mean I did apologize, and it wasn't like I had done this to her before. I wasn't sure what had just taken place but I was sure that Wanda would get over it. Then again, if she didn't, I still had Tre and that was all that mattered.

Chapter 15

Two weeks had passed, and Wanda and I had not spoken since the day I stood her up. I missed her tremendously, but I couldn't bring myself to go back and face her. I knew that I had really disappointed her, but my obsession with Tre outweighed everything else.

I told him about our falling out, and he told me that I really didn't need to go apartment hunting.

"You can move in with me," he stated simply, like that was the only logical thing for me to do. "My roommate is in and out of the country a lot, so I pretty much have the place to myself. Besides he won't mind." Needless to say, I was elated and didn't waste any time getting my stuff ready to go.

It didn't take me long to pack, since I only had my clothes and a couple of other personal items that I had accrued during my year there. After everything had been cleared out, I took a deep breath and made my way to the office to turn in my key.

When I entered, I rang the bell and waited for Wanda to come to the front. She poked her head out to see who it was and then disappeared. Just when I had decided to leave the key on the counter and call it a day, she sauntered up to the counter and looked at me expectantly.

"So...what can I do for you?" she asked pointedly.

"I...I just wanted to let you know that I found a place and I need to turn in my key," I said quietly.

"Oh..." she replied, as she snatched my key up off the counter. I caught the sad look on her face as she tried to turn away and hide it. "So where you movin' to?"

I hesitated briefly before I responded, "Tre is letting me move into his place."

There was a long uncomfortable silence as she stared at me in disbelief. I was so ashamed of myself at that moment that I couldn't stand there any longer and bear her accusing gaze. "I'll go now," I said, as I turned to leave.

"Sugarpie, wait," she called coming from around the counter, "listen...don't go. Let's think this through. That man ain't nothin' but trouble and I don't want to see you get hurt. Please..."

I looked her in the eye and swallowed the lump that was forming in my throat. I didn't want to hurt Wanda. She was the only friend I had in the world, but she didn't understand what I was going through. I loved Tre with every fiber of my being and if she couldn't accept that then I was going to have to prepare myself to let her go and that hurt me deeply.

"Wanda," I began taking a deep breath, "there is nothing you can say to make me change my mind about this, so please don't try. I love him and I don't care if he's married. He told me that he loves me and is leaving her. I believe him. If he didn't love me then he wouldn't be moving me into his house. Now I love you and I appreciate everything that you have done for me, but if you can't get past this then… we can't be friends anymore. I'm sorry." And with that, I walked out the door and did not look back.

As I walked away, I could feel Wanda's shocked stare burning on my back, but I held my head high and walked straight to Tre's car and got in.

He smiled at me and said, "You ready?"

I looked him in the eye and smiled as I nodded my head. I was ready and willing to follow him wherever he wanted to lead me.

Chapter 16

I don't think my feet touched the floor the entire time that we were carrying my things into the apartment. I was so tickled because I had visions dancing around in my head of me cooking dinner for Tre after work, and then wearing little skimpy nighties to bed for him at night. The possibilities of what we could do were endless and I couldn't wait to get settled in, so that we could start playing house.

Things were perfect for the first couple of weeks. He made me feel like his whole life revolved around making me happy. We cooked dinner together, stayed up watching movies till the wee hours of the morning, and had more sex than ever. He indulged my childish fantasies for a while and then reality set in.

"Timber," he called from the front room suddenly, "I'm goin' out for awhile."

"Where are you going?" I inquired, as I came running from the back.

"Out! Why don't you do something constructive, like clean some shit or something," he snapped, as he walked out and slammed the door behind him.

I stood there staring at the closed door with a blank look on my face. I tried not to get upset, so I told myself that he was probably just going out with his boys for a while.

"It's not good for him to be sitting up under me all the time anyway," I told myself. I was still trying to sell myself that same story when he came strolling in at three 'o clock in the morning.

"Where have you been, Tre?" I whined, "I was worried. You could've called or something."

"Look, don't start that naggin' shit. I told you I was going out and that is all you need to know. Ok?" he shot out pointedly.

"Ok," I said with hot tears stinging my eyes. I couldn't believe that he was talking to me like that.

"You don't have to be nasty. How would you feel if I came strollin' in at three o'clock in the morning?"

His look softened and he came and hugged me tight. "I'm sorry, baby...it's just that you reminded me of the ex-wife just then and I just got a little aggravated. She used to grill me all the time and I hated that," he explained, as he planted kisses on my neck.

"I'm sorry."

"It's ok. How about if I take you to the movies tomorrow to make it up to you?"

"Ok," I said perking up immediately.

The next day marked the day of our first official fight. We left work, and after grabbing a bite to eat we went straight to the movies. After the show, as we were walking out he excused himself to go to the bathroom. While I stood there waiting for him to come out, a handsome man who looked to be about Tre's age approached me with a smile.

"How you doin'?" he asked politely.

"Fine," I replied nervously looking around for Tre.

"I just had to come over here and tell you how absolutely beautiful you are. Are you here with someone?" he asked smiling.

"Yes, I am," I said blushing.

"He's a lucky man. Well…you have a nice night ok?" he replied and walked away.

I stared at the floor until I was sure that he was gone and when I looked up Tre was standing in front of me, with a look of pure rage on his face.

"Who the fuck was that?" he spat. I didn't know what to say. I was startled by his outburst, so I just stood there and stared at him in disbelief. "Did you hear me?"

"I don't know! Just some guy that was trying to talk to me. What is your problem?"

He didn't say a word as he grabbed my arm and pulled me to the car. We drove in silence as I stared at him trying to figure out why he was acting like that. He was acting like he had caught me having sex with the man in the lobby!

When we got home, as soon as we got into the house and closed the door I found myself being thrown up against the wall with his hand around my neck

"Now, I'm only gonna ask you this one more time, Timberlynn...who the fuck was that man you were talking to?" he snarled, with his face only inches from mine.

I could hardly breathe as I struggled to release his hand from my neck but he was too strong. "Answer me?" he yelled.

"I don't know him," I choked, as tears streamed down my face, "he asked me if I was there with someone and I said yes"

"You'd better not be lying to me, girl. I told you...you belong to me now. If I ever catch you with another man, I can't even tell you what I would do to you. Do you understand?" I didn't answer right away, because I could feel myself getting light headed, so he squeezed harder. "Answer me."

"Yes," I gasped with all the breath I could muster.

"Good," he said loosening his grip on my neck. I slid down to the floor sobbing and I could feel him standing over me. He knelt down and began to stroke my hair softly.

"I'm sorry, baby...I didn't mean to scare you. Look at me...," he whispered, as he pulled me up to face him, "I love you, Timber, I just don't know what came over me...when I saw that guy talking to you I just lost it. I'm sorry..." he apologized over and over as he planted kisses all over my face.

I remember wondering, as I sat there rocking myself back and forth, what had I gotten myself into.

One thing I knew for sure was that I didn't have anywhere else to go.

Chapter 17

After that incident, things went from bad to worse. Tre began to monitor all of my activities at work. He would get mad if he even thought I was looking at another man the wrong way. I couldn't even be in the presence of someone he thought I might find attractive. He would halfway catch an attitude if Mr. Griffin talked to me for what he thought was too long. When no one was looking, I would receive a hard pinch on the butt as a reminder that he was watching me.

But on the other hand, his flirting went on like business as usual. I couldn't stand it anymore so one night I confronted him when we got home.

"Why do you do that?" I shot out at him.

"What are you talking about?" he asked, as though he really didn't have a clue as to what I meant.

"You get mad at me for things that you make up in your head about me doing with other men, but then you turn right around and flirt with those women right in my face!" I fired, "Why?"

"I keep telling you that flirting is my job. Don't you like having nice things and living in a place like this? Well it ain't free. I gotta get paid and the way I get paid is by making women feel pretty, so that they will continue to pay me. You on the other hand…your job doesn't require you to talk to anyone," he replied matter-of-factly, "scrubbing toilets doesn't require talking or talent of any kind."

"You think you are so smart, Tre. You just wait," I retorted, stung by his remark.

"Don't be jealous," he said teasingly, as he kissed me playfully. "Hey listen, I gotta run out for a little bit, so have dinner ready when I get back, ok."

"Ok," I said sullenly.

He left and I spent the remainder of the night preparing the perfect meal for him to come home to, only to sit up waiting for him until eleven thirty; five hours later. I was fit to be tied.

"Where have you been?"

"Don't worry about it," he shot back.

"You know what, Tre, I am sick of this shit! I'm tired of you treating me like some little puppy instead of your live in girlfriend! I sat here and busted my ass cooking for you and you didn't even have the decency to call me and tell me you would be home late. Then I call and you don't answer your phone?" I screamed.

"Ok, Timber…do you really want to know where I was?" he asked calmly. "I was over to my ex-wife's house having a long conversation with her. Ok? Is that what you want to hear?"

I felt like I had just been kicked in my stomach. "What?" I asked astonished.

"What do you mean 'what'? You heard what I said. I'm going through a divorce, and I will occasionally have to deal with Brooke. Get used to it," he threw back, as he walked to the bedroom and slammed the door.

I just sat there on the couch and tried to take in what he had just said. Tears sprung to my eyes as I tried to swallow the lump in my throat.

"Don't cry," I told myself, "It makes sense...I guess." Did it? I tried to put it out of my mind and decided to go and apologize. I didn't want to be one of those nagging women, so I pulled myself together and went to the bedroom to talk to him but the door was locked.

I knocked softly and called, "Tre...open the door." There was only silence so I knocked again. "Tre...please unlock the door."

"No," he called back, "you sleep on the couch tonight."

"You can't be serious..." I laughed.

All of a sudden, he snatched the door open and said, "Either you sleep on the couch or you can get the fuck out! Those are your two choices." I just stood there searching his face trying to understand why he was treating me this way.

When I realized that he was serious, I went to the closet, grabbed some blankets, and walked back to the couch. I sat in the darkness for a long time trying to get my head together.

At that moment, I missed Wanda so much and the sadness was so overwhelming that I felt sick to my stomach. Before I knew it, I had the phone in my hand

and was dialing her number. Before I hit the final digit I hung up.

I couldn't call her. What would she think? What would she say after how I had treated her? I was at a total loss and didn't know what to do, so I just lay there and cried myself to sleep.

The next morning when I woke up, Tre was already gone. I went into the kitchen to fix myself some breakfast and found a note posted on the refrigerator that read, "I'm sorry. Please forgive me." I snatched the note off and threw it in the garbage with disgust.

"Bastard," I grumbled to myself, as I went to the back to get dressed for work. As I opened the door to leave, I saw a huge basket sitting on the floor filled with the most beautiful flowers I had ever seen. All my anger immediately melted away, as I picked up the card and tore it open with excitement. "I love you, please forgive me" was neatly printed on the inside. In that instant I forgave him for everything.

When I walked into work, I was practically singing I was so happy. I hated it when we fought, but the thought of making up made butterflies flutter in my stomach. I punched in and went to Tre's office to let him know that I loved the flowers but he wasn't there. So then I went to the front desk and asked the receptionist if she had seen him.

"No, he hasn't made it in yet," she said.

"Oh...ok," I said trying to hide my disappointment. I wondered where he could possibly be, but then I stopped myself. Today was going to be a good day; I was bound and determined. I would not question him when I saw him and I would not have an attitude.

"If this relationship is going to work, I am going to have to start trusting him," I told myself.

When he did finally stroll in, he casually cornered me in the locker room and asked, "Did you miss this last night?"

"No! You got a lot of nerve..." I said taking a playful swing at him. He dodged it easily, spun me around, and hugged me from behind.

"You wanna do it right here?" he whispered in my ear.

"Tre, stop it before we both get fired," I said in a hushed voice, as he started kissing on my neck. I struggled to get away from him at first, for fear of getting caught, but soon I was responding passionately to his kisses. Suddenly the door flew open and Korey came barging in.

"Oh...my bad," she retorted with an amused look on her face.

"Well, I better be going," said Tre, as he walked toward the door. "Sup, Korey."

"Yeah, what's up is right," she replied staring at me. "Uh,huh..."

"Whatever..." I said brushing past her. I was not in the mood to hear her mouth.

The day couldn't have gone by fast enough, because I couldn't wait to get home and make up with

Tre. I ran to the locker room to get my stuff and as I was working the combination on my lock, all of a sudden my head was slammed into the locker. My mind reeled as I was spun around and slammed again. I saw blackness for a moment. When I came to, I was on the floor and Brooke was standing over me with a crazed look on her face.

"Get up, bitch!" she said menacingly, as she bent down and pulled me up by my hair. "Who do you think you are fucking with? Do you really think that I am going to let you steal my husband from me? You'd better watch your back, bitch!" she spat and then socked me in the face. I fell to the floor holding my face crying.

"Please...," I sobbed, "stop..."

"What do you mean stop?" she laughed, as if my pleading was the funniest thing she had ever heard. "I haven't even gotten started. If I see you around my husband again, I am going to fuck you up, do you hear me?"

I was too shaken to respond, so I just lay there and prayed that she wouldn't hit me again. Apparently that satisfied her because she spun on her heels and walked out.

I'm not sure how long I lay there before I was able to pull myself together. I dragged myself off the floor and walked to the mirror to assess the damage. I looked pretty bad. My left eye was puffy, my lip was split, and there was a knot on the back of my head that felt like it was growing by the minute.

Walking out like this was out of the question. I didn't want anyone to see me that way, so I sat back down and tried to collect my thoughts. After about ten minutes, I gathered my belongings and crept out the backdoor.

When I got home, Tre took one look at my face and went into hysterics. "Who did this to you?" he raged.

I laughed in spite of myself. "Your wife. Apparently she doesn't want me to see you anymore," I replied sarcastically, as I fell on the couch exhausted.

"Timber..." he said sadly touching my face softly, "I am so sorry she did this to you. Don't worry, I'll take care of everything." He got up and snatched up his jacket and made his way toward the door.

"Wait...where are you going?" I asked frantically.

"To find Brooke."

"No! Are you crazy? Who knows what she'll do to me next time if you say something to her!"

"Timberlynn, look at your face! What the fuck? You expect me to just sit here and do nothing," he asked angrily.

"Yes...please don't go. Just stay here with me ok?" I pleaded.

He stared at me for a long moment, then his face softened and he dropped his coat on the floor and rejoined me on the couch. Just being close to him made me feel safe again.

"I won't go now, but you better believe that I'm going to deal with this…soon," he promised.

It scared me to even think about what kind of problems that would bring about for me in the near future. One thing that I was certain of was that I would find out sooner than later.

Chapter 18

Two weeks passed following the locker room incident and things had gotten pretty much back to normal. My war wounds healed, but I began taking a lot of precautions in my daily routine to make sure that Brooke didn't creep up on me again.

No longer did I store my belongings in the locker room; instead I packed a duffel bag and kept it under the reception desk. When I had to use the bathroom, I used the client locker room, and always when there were a lot of people in it.

The situation at home was better than it had been in a long time. I think that Tre felt bad about what Brooke had done to me, so he was very hesitant to leave me alone. He was back to being the way he was when we first started living together.

One Saturday I woke up in bed alone, so I laid there basking in the sunlight that was shining on my face. I didn't really want to get up because I had a weird feeling in the pit of my stomach. It was already twelve thirty, so I figured I should get up and do something constructive with my day off.

After forcing myself out of bed, I went to the kitchen and found a note on the table from Tre stating that he would be back shortly. I fixed myself a cup of coffee and sat deep in thought.

Out of nowhere, a feeling of complete loneliness washed over me. I found myself staring at the phone wondering what my parents were doing. Did they miss me even a little? Were they worried about me? I had been gone over a year and a half, without a word or letter to them. It broke my heart to think that the answer to any of my questions may have been no.

Before I could sink too deep into my depression, I heard Tre's keys in the lock. Trying to appear normal, I jumped up and started cleaning the kitchen.

"Hey," he said walking in.

"Hey," I replied running over to kiss him, but he turned his face away so that my kiss landed on his cheek. Clearly something was very wrong. I searched his face for signs but he would not look me in the eye, instead he took me by the hand, led me to the table, and sat down next to me.

"What's wrong?"

"Timber, I have something to tell you and I really don't know how to say it. So...I guess the best thing to do is to just come out and say it," he said sadly.

"Tre, what is it? Are you ok?" I asked, with tears welling up in my eyes. From the look on his face, I knew that what he was about to say was not going to be good.

He didn't say anything for what seemed like forever, instead he just sat there playing with my hands as if he didn't know how to begin.

"Timberlynn... you know that I love you, right?"

"Yes..." I replied nervously.

"This thing with my wife is turning out to be a lot harder than I thought it would be. See...after she did what she did to you I went over there to straighten her out. But then we got to talking and I realized that there is still a lot that we haven't tried to do in order to save our marriage..." he began. As the words were still coming out of his mouth, I could feel myself getting sicker and sicker by the moment.

"No...I'm not hearing this right now, Tre," I said jumping up from the table and running into the bedroom. I could hear his footsteps behind me as I tried to escape whatever it was he was trying to tell me.

He grabbed my arm and spun me around so that I was facing him and then sat me down.

"Timber, you need to listen to what I am trying to tell you! Do you think that this is easy for me? I have been out all morning trying to figure out how to do this!"

I snatched my arms away from him with more strength than I knew I had, and pushed him backward. "What!" I screamed, "Are you going to tell me that you're leaving me and going back to your wife? Is that what's so hard for you to say, Tre? Is that what the fuck you're trying to tell me?"

He said nothing as he sat there staring at me like I was crazy.

"Answer me!" I yelled.

"Yes," he said sadly.

After that, I came unglued. I jumped on him and starting slapping and punching with reckless abandon. He was caught totally off guard by my attack, so all he could do was try to protect his face from my vicious blows.

"You bastard," I cried hysterically still throwing blows, "how could you do this to me? I gave up everything for you and now you're telling me that you're going back to your wife?"

With one final swing, I landed a vicious blow to his nose and blood flew everywhere. That was the final straw, as he finally decided to defend himself. The next thing I knew, I was being slammed on the floor and pinned down with my arms above my head.

"Listen to me," he said calmly, "if you hit me again I am going to break your arms. Do you hear me?"

I immediately stopped struggling and glared at him.

"Now, this is what's going to happen… I'm going back home and I'm giving you two weeks to get your stuff together and get out of here. I am really sorry to do this to you, but you can't stay here. I will do what I can to help you find a place." He studied me to see what my reaction would be, but I just lay there glaring. He loosened his grip on my arms and asked, "Are you calmed down now so I can let you go?"

"Yes," I spat as he let me go, I jumped up and headed for the closet.

"Where are you going?"

"I don't need you to give me two weeks to do anything! I will get my shit and leave right now. I'm not staying here one more day! I can't be where I'm not wanted...not now, not ever again," I cried.

My heart was broken. First my parents didn't want me and now him. As I dashed from one place to the next, packing my things in a duffel bag, I tried to figure out what I was going to do. I didn't have any place to go except back to Wanda, and Lord only knew what she was going to say. But one thing was for sure...I would not and could not be in this place for a minute longer.

"Timberlynn, just stop. You don't have anywhere else to go. In spite of everything I do care what happens to you. Please...don't leave like this. Stay here so we can find you someplace where you'll be ok."

I didn't respond as I continued to gather my things. When I finally finished, I slung my bag over my shoulder and headed for the door. Just as my hand reached for the knob, I felt his hand on my shoulder and I stopped.

"Please don't leave like this...I'm sorry. I never meant to hurt you, Timberlynn."

My whole body went ridged as I felt the warmth of his hand on me. I wanted to turn around and hug him and beg him to stay with me, but the little bit of pride that I had left would not allow it. I knew that I had to leave him and never look back. Wanda had warned me and I didn't listen, so now I was being punished. Being strong was the only option.

"Goodbye, Tre," I said and walked out the door. I could feel his eyes on me as I walked away, but I was determined not to look back. Even as I hit the button on the elevator I managed to keep from meeting his gaze as the door closed. Once the elevator began its descent, I fell into another round of heart wrenching sobs.

I had no idea what I was going to do next.

Chapter 19

Karma is a huge and intimidating beast of a thing I thought to myself, as I stood outside of the motel office door trying to make my feet move. I knew that Wanda was in there watching television because I had peeked inside and saw the back of her head. Never in a million years, would I have thought that it would be this hard to walk through her door, but I didn't have anywhere else to go.

So finally, I said a silent prayer and then went inside to get it over with. Either she would welcome me with open arms or she would curse me out and send me on my merry way.

I rang the bell on the counter and braced myself for the worse as she turned around to see who it was. When she saw me, her face immediately lit up as she rushed around the counter and hugged me tightly.

At first, I didn't react because her reaction caught me completely off guard. Anger was what I was ready for. I wanted her to yell and scream at me for treating her the way that I did, but instead she held me at arms length and said, "Sweetie, I'm so glad you came back! I was so worried about you that I haven't slept one sound night since you been gone."

Immediately, the tears began to fall and I was spilling my whole miserable story to her. By the time

I'd finished talking, I was shaking and heaving uncontrollably from all the crying I had done.

Wanda didn't say a word the entire time that I was explaining what happened. She just listened intently. When I told her the part about Brooke attacking me in the locker room, her face hardened and she gritted her teeth but still said nothing.

"Alright now, Sugarpie, don't you worry about nothin'. You're safe now. I'll get you back up in your room and we'll figure out what to do in the morning. Ok?" she said, helping me up.

I allowed her to lead me to my room where she helped me out of my clothes and into bed. Unconsciousness followed immediately after. I woke up the next morning at about one o'clock in the afternoon and just lay in the bed, until I heard a soft knock on the door.

"Timberlynn...are you up?" Wanda called softly.

I hopped out of the bed and opened the door. "Hi."

"Good morning...or afternoon I should say," she replied, as she came in and shut the door.

"Look, Wanda," I began, "I owe you a huge apology..."

"You don't have to..."

"No, please let me finish," I interrupted. "You have been nothing but nice to me since I came to Detroit...and how I treated you was wrong and I am so sorry. You were right all along and I am sorrier than you will ever know that I didn't listen to you. Can you ever find it in your heart to forgive me?"

"Oh, baby, of course I do," she sighed, as she got up and hugged me. "You're like a daughter to me and all I want is for you to be happy. All is forgiven. Just promise me that you will leave that man alone."

"I promise," I said. The bad thing is that in my heart I really meant it.

Chapter 20

"Oh no!" I yelled, as I slammed the pregnancy test down on the counter. "Please, God, no, no, no..." Angry tears streamed down my face, as I paced around the bathroom.

"I know, I'll take all of them...if one of them says negative then I'll be ok," I reasoned out loud.

I snatched the two remaining pregnancy tests out of the box and sat them on the counter next to the positive one. Then I drank about a gallon of water and waited for the urge to come. Finally, after about fifteen minutes I was sure I could force myself to pee so I took both tests at the same time. The next three minutes were torture as I waited for them to reveal my results.

"Holy, mother of..." I swore, as I held up the two last tests and observed the pink lines slowly starting to appear. "What am I going to do now?"

I was a week late for my period and I had been throwing up left and right. At first, I thought it might have been the flu, but when Wanda told me that I should go get a test, I took her advice right away. I usually never got sick, so I knew that something had to be wrong.

Nothing could have prepared me for this! It had been about three weeks since I moved out of Tre's house and thus far, I had no contact with him whatsoever. I managed to avoid him completely at work, even though I was told on several occasions that he had asked about me. Now I find out that I am pregnant with his baby?!

I picked up the phone and called Wanda and she came over right away. By the time she got to my room, I was inconsolable.

"Listen, you have got to pull yourself together. This is not the end of the world. You still have choices here."

"What do you mean choices, Wanda? I can't kill no baby and I can't raise a child by myself!" I wailed.

"Well those are your choices, Sugarpie. Women do it all the time. Having a child is not the end of the world. You are just going to have to make some sacrifices, that's all," she said knowingly.

I was so beside myself with grief that I couldn't even speak; I just sat there and cried until I had nothing left. Wanda said nothing. She just rocked gently back and forth and stroked my hair.

Right at that second I had a moment of clarity: I was not going to have this baby alone. I would go to work tomorrow, march right up to Tre, tell him I was pregnant, and make him take care of his responsibility. Maybe this was what we needed to get us back on the right track! He was clearly confused if he thought that he should stay with Brooke, because obviously she wasn't making him happy. Once I told him the news, he would see his mistake and we could start all over and begin planning for our family.

I smiled at the possibility, as I continued to let Wanda rock me and stroke my hair. I would tell her about my idea after I talked to Tre. Surely, she would understand my reasons for wanting to make things work with the father of my child. After all, she was a mother too.

The next day at work, I nervously rehearsed how I was going to break the news to Tre. My stomach was churning and I started to feel sick, but I was determined not to leave that floor until I had a chance to talk to him. I was not about to risk missing his entrance because I was in the bathroom tossing my cookies.

Unfortunately, the baby that was growing inside of me won the battle. After taking one whiff of the cleaning solution I had opened, I had to make a mad dash into the ladies room.

Korey came in right behind me with a concerned look on her face. "Timerlynn, are you ok?" she asked.

"Yeah," I panted, as I gripped the toilet, "I think I'm coming down with something, that's all."

"Ok, well do you need any help?"

"No. I'll be ok. Thank you," I said gratefully. I hadn't been very kind to Korey and she had always been nice to me. I made a mental note to apologize to her before I left work today.

Once I was back on the floor again, I noticed that Tre's door was closed. That meant that he had slipped in while I was in the bathroom. I gathered my courage and knocked on his door.

"Come in," he called.

I opened the door slowly and stuck my head in to make sure that he was alone. "Can I talk to you?"

"Yeah, have a seat," he responded. "It'll have to be quick, I have a client coming in at eleven."

I sat down, wiped the sweat off my palms, and tried to decide the best way to come right out and say it. All of a sudden, the speech that I had been practicing all morning didn't seem to fit.

"What's up, Timberlynn?"

Just spit it out I told myself. "Tre...I'm pregnant." There I'd said it. It felt like a huge weight had been taken off my shoulders.

"And? What are you telling me for?"

"What do you mean what am I telling you for?" I asked in disbelief. "It's yours!"

"How do I know that?" he snarled. I couldn't believe that he could sit there and say that to me!

"You know it's yours, Tre! Don't even try to play me like that!"

"Look, Timberlynn...let's say for argument's sake that it is mine, what do you want me to do about it?" he asked callously. "I already told you that I am trying to work things out with my wife, so I'm sure that you know that a baby by another woman would complicate things."

"I just thought..."

"You thought what? You thought you would drop this on me and I would change my mind about everything? Then we could be a happy family? Is that what you thought?" he snapped.

"I thought you would be happy. I guess..." I trailed off.

"That's the problem, Timber, you don't think. I swear you dumb bitches!"

"What?!" I gasped.

"You listen to me... you'd better not have this baby, Timber, or you will be very, very sorry. Do you understand?" he said menacingly.

When I didn't respond, he came from around his desk and backed me up against the wall. Angrily, he cupped my face in his hands and roughly squeezed my cheeks together. "Do you hear me?"

I snatched my face away and slid from under him and yelled, "I am not having an abortion...I don't care what you say!"

"Yes, I think you will if you know what's good for you. Now..." he began, as he pulled a wad of money out of his pocket and shoved it into my hand, "here's three hundred dollars. That should be enough to get it taken care of. I don't want to have this conversation again." With that he pushed me to the side and walked out.

I just stood there staring at the wad of cash in my hand. Things had not gone the way I planned them at all. Brooke had obviously brainwashed him and poisoned him against me.

He did love me…he had told me so many times that I was his. You don't just tell someone you love them as many times as he did and not mean it. I just had to find a way to make him realize that I was the one that he needed to be with, not her. In time, he would see that he wanted this baby as much as I now did.

Chapter 21

I must have called Tre's phone at least a hundred times, but he wouldn't answer. Finally, on my hundred and fifth call, I decided to leave a message.

"Tre," I sobbed, "why are you doing this to me? I love you and I know you love me! I am not having an abortion and I don't want to raise our child alone, so please call me so we can talk about this. Please."

Two hours went by, as I sat by the phone and waited for him to call me back. I was beside myself with grief. My heart was racing and my head was pounding in my ears. The depression I felt was so overwhelming that I found myself sitting on the bathroom floor, with a razor in my hand.

As I sat there rocking back and forth, different scenes kept playing over and over in my mind; us laughing, us holding hands in the park, us making love. I smiled to myself as I thought about the first time we kissed and the first time he told me that he loved me.

Tears of frustration and disgust streamed down my face, as I saw myself watching myself from somewhere else in the room. It was as if I had left my body and was watching my grief-stricken self on the bathroom floor, with razor in hand poised to make the first deadly strike, and the me that was watching was powerless to stop it.

"What are you doing?" I tried to scream at myself, but self wasn't listening. Self was tired of being unloved and unwanted. Self was sick of being alone. Self loved Tre and didn't want to live anymore if she couldn't have him.

I felt that first wave of pain race through my body, as I cut the first layer of skin on my left wrist. I threw my head back to let it seep in. I hadn't done that in a long time but the old familiar feeling overtook me instantly. I was in a painful euphoria that allowed me to release the pain mounting inside of me. I savored it, as I watched the blood ooze down my arm.

"There it is…" I murmured. I don't know how much time passed, while I soaked up the pain in my left arm, but I was starting to feel woozy. "Uh, oh," I said looking at my right arm, "I didn't forget about you."

Putting the razor in my left hand, I pinched it between my fingers and tried to steady it for the final cut. It was a little difficult because my fingers were getting numb. I finally managed to get a decent grip on the razor so I could run my right wrist over it. That cut went deep…really deep.

The razor fell from my hand and I sat there and waited for blessed sleep to come. It was really weird, I remember thinking to myself, because my vision got dark from the outside in. Blackness crept in like shadows moving across a room, moving in from the sides and ending in the middle. I don't even remember going to sleep, but I do remember my final thought being, "I wonder what Heaven will be like?"

Chapter 22

"Sugarpie, wake up," I heard Wanda calling softly. "You wake up, now. It ain't time for you to leave here yet," she said, as I felt her hand moving softly across my hair. I tried to open my eyes and tell her that I was ok, but they were too heavy.

"I'm sorry, ma'am, but I am going to have to ask you to step outside for a moment. We have to change her I.V.," I heard a woman's voice say.

"Ok. Sugarpie, I'm gon' have to step out for a minute but I'll be right outside that door, ok? I'll come back as soon as they finish," Wanda promised.

After a moment, I felt a slight tugging on my arm, as the lady started doing whatever it was she had to do and then I was alone again. I tried again to open my eyes and this time a little bit of light seeped under my eyelids. It felt as if someone had glued my eyes shut, and suddenly, I started to panic. Why couldn't I open my eyes? What was wrong with me?

Then it hit me. I had tried to kill myself and failed. Now I was in the hospital and my eyes didn't work. It didn't seem like I could do anything right. With one final act of will, I tried again and this time they opened and the brightness of the florescent lights forced me to close them again.

As I lay there trying to get my eyes to adjust, Wanda came back in and smiled when she saw that I was awake.

"Oh, baby, I'm so glad you're awake! You almost gave me a heart attack! I never saw so much blood in my life. What were you thinkin'?" she gushed, as she hugged me and wiped the tears from her eyes.

"I don't know," I choked looking at the wall. I couldn't look her in the face because I felt so stupid.

"You don't know? Well…we'll leave that alone for right now, I'm just glad to see that you didn't succeed at whatever it was you was trying to do."

"How long have I been in here?" I asked.

"Two days."

"Is the baby ok?"

"Fortunately, yes, praise God. You been blessed, girl. Doctor says you lucky because if you would've cut any deeper on that right arm, you would've lost all use of it. Would that have made you happy, Timber?"

"No, it would have made me happy to be dead!" I snapped.

"You better stop talkin' like that or these people gone have you committed, you hear me? Now, I managed to get the doctor to agree to release you into my care when you get discharged because I promised him that you wasn't going to try this nonsense again. Not on my watch," Wanda said, looking pointedly at me, "now you go on and rest up so we can get you home. And when I say home…I mean my house, where I can keep a good eye on you."

I didn't see the point in arguing with her so I just lay there staring at the ceiling. After a week of observation and a bunch of tests, the doctor was finally convinced that I wasn't going to try to kill myself again anytime soon, so I was allowed to leave the hospital. Wanda drove me straight to her house and set me up in her guestroom.

"I've asked my aunt to come over here and sit with you when I have to work, but I cut my hours so that shouldn't be very often. Are you feeling ok?"

I nodded my head.

"Timberlynn, you have got to snap out of this. No man is worth all this. You gon' be a mama, so you better get it together for the sake of this child. That man is married, so you need to move on and leave him alone."

"I know," I agreed tearfully. She just didn't understand that it was easier said than done. Now I knew that he didn't love me because he didn't even bother to come and see me at the hospital. He had to have known I was there because Wanda had called my job to let them know that I'd had an accident. I could have died for all he knew.

"We are going to get through this together, you hear me? You'll be back on your feet in no time," she promised, as she patted my leg.

She was right. I was back on my feet in no time. The next week I was back to work as if nothing happened. Mr. Griffin was very gracious and allowed me to return without asking me a million questions.

No one knew why I was in the hospital and I wasn't about to tell them. I made up an elaborate story about how I tripped and fell down some stairs and cracked my ribs. Everyone was very sympathetic, including Tre.

He called me into his office and shut the door.

"Is everything all right?" he inquired with a look of concern on his face, which I found very amusing.

"What's it matter to you?"

"I heard you were in the hospital. Did you get that taken care of?"

"You mean did I kill our child, Tre? No...I didn't. Is that all you called me in here for?" I asked as calmly as I could.

"No, I really was worried about you," he said coming around the desk to hold my hands,

"You know I still care about you. But, I'm sure you can understand why I couldn't come and see you. Brooke won't let me out of her sight," he complained, as he kissed me softly. "I miss you."

"Really?" I asked uncertainly. I didn't trust him but seeing him right then made me weak. I wanted him so bad I could taste it.

"Really, really," he murmured, as he stroked my face and then kissed me deeply. I fell in readily, as I returned his kisses with a hunger that was frightening. Then I came to my senses and pulled away from him.

"What's wrong?"

I didn't say a word as I rushed out of the office.

Later that night, I lay in my bed staring at the ceiling while my mind raged. I felt like I had to do something to make him feel like I felt. I was torn between loving him and hating him all at the same time. Then I remembered the three hundred dollars he had given me for the abortion that he ordered me to get.

I jumped up and ran over to my drawer and pulled it out, then just sat there looking thoughtfully at it. Before I knew it, I was outside the motel approaching one of the prostitutes that I saw out there every night.

"Well, well, well…what can I do for you?" she asked smiling.

"I need to know where I can buy a gun."

"Oh," she said looking disappointed, "I thought you might've been ready to get turned out, young one. Anyway, what do you need a gun for?"

"Protection," I said quickly.

She looked at me for a long moment and then said, "Yeah, ok. How much you got to spend?"

"Three hundred."

"I'll see what I can do," she replied and then walked off.

A few hours later, she was knocking on the door with my new handgun. Well, it wasn't new but it would work. It was a small revolver that fit snuggly right into the palm of my hand. I marveled at the sudden surge of power I felt, as I turned it around in my hand.

"It's empty," she said digging into her purse and coming up with a hand full of bullets, "but I made him gimme some shells."

"Here," she said shoving them into my other hand, "Now do you know how to use that thing?"

"Yeah," I said, as I shoved the money into her out stretched hand and shut the door in her face.

I sat down and opened the chamber of the gun and stared at it for a long time. The blackness inside held me captive. Slowly I began to push the bullets into the holes and once they were filled, I pushed it closed and fingered the safety. I had watched my dad plenty of times, so I was pretty sure that I knew how to handle a gun.

In my mind, I couldn't go wrong with a gun the next time I got the notion to leave this world. I was fairly sure that I still wanted to, just wasn't sure that now was the time. Part of me really wanted to stay and have this baby, so that I could experience what it would be like to have someone really love me. The other part was just tired of being disappointed. I really didn't know how much longer I could continue to live with the fact that the man I loved belonged to someone else.

One thing was for sure… I wasn't going to make it easy for him.

Chapter 23

I didn't recognize the girl who was rummaging through Tre's office trying to find his address. All I knew was that the girl's hands looked an awful lot like mine, when I looked down at them to read the street number on the piece of paper that she held. Not only was this girl boldly going through Tre's office, but she was actually standing in front of Korey fixing her lips to say something crazy.

"Korey," I heard my voice say coming out of her mouth, "do you think you could give me a ride somewhere after work?"

"Where?" she asked.

"I have to pick up something from a friend's house," I heard myself say.

"It's not going to take long is it?"

"No, I'll only be a few minutes."

"Yeah, I can do that," she agreed.

As I walked to the back to get my purse, I felt my heart racing inside my chest. I could not believe what I was about to do. Was I really about to go to Tre's house, the house that he shared with his wife, and demand that he acknowledge me and the fact that we were going to have a baby? This was not me at all. This was the girl that I saw in the mirror the first night that we went out; the bold and confident girl that wasn't going to take no for an answer.

Who did he think he was dealing with? Did he think he could just use me and then throw me away like a used dishrag? These were the questions that were screaming in my mind as Korey pulled up to the address I had given her.

After Korey killed the engine, I sat in the passenger seat and stared out the window at their house. Her house. It was a nice big house with a perfectly manicured lawn and picture perfect window dressings. It was the perfect house for a family. Our family. I was the one that should have been with him in that house! Not her! I could feel my rage growing more and more by the second.

"I'll be right back," I told Korey, as I got out of the car and slammed the door. It was almost as if I was watching the whole thing take place from outside of myself. I just really couldn't believe that it was me doing what I was clearly about to do. Before I could stop myself, I was banging on the door with reckless abandon.

"Just a minute!" I could hear Brooke call out from inside. As I listened to the locks disengage, I stood on the other side with my fists clenched. Seconds later, I was standing face to face with the woman who had assaulted me only a few weeks before.

"What the fuck?!" she gasped in surprise.
"Where is Tre?" I asked fearlessly.

"No this bitch is not standing on my porch asking where my husband is!" she laughed in disbelief.

"Just tell him that I'm here. We have unfinished ..." I began and before I could finish my sentence, I was caught with a swift jab to the nose.

My eyes watered as my hands flew to my face and I felt warm sticky blood begin to course down my lips. Blind rage is what came next. It was like I came out of my body again and saw my screaming self grab Brooke by the ears and drive her back into the house. I then cut loose and began swinging blindly at her like a starved child trying to free candy from a piñata.

The rest was a blur but the last thing I remember was Korey grabbing me and dragging me back to her car kicking and screaming.

"Come on! We gotta get outta here before the police come!" she screamed at me. At that point I sobered right up and jumped into the car just in time to keep my legs from being ripped off as she took off down the street. In the rearview mirror, I could see Brooke running toward the car as we drove off.

"What the fuck were you doing over there, Timber! What are you trying to do? Get us both killed? You trick me into bringing you to Tre's house, so you can beat up his wife? What the hell is wrong with you?" she shrieked. Her hands were shaking as she tried to steer the car and calm herself down.

I didn't respond. Adrenaline was still pumping through my body at warp speed and I didn't feel like explaining myself right then.

"Oh my gosh, ohmigosh, ohmigosh…" she repeated over and over, as she drove and surveyed the rearview mirror.

"Look, Korey, I didn't mean for that to happen," I began shakily, "I just wanted to talk to Tre and she hit me. She started it."

"Well what the hell did you expect? You went to the woman's house looking for her husband! Do you understand that? Her husband! Did you think she was going to open the door and invite you in for tea? You are one crazy bitch, you know that?" she replied. "I can't believe you got me involved in this shit!"

"I'm pregnant," I blurted out.

The car skidded to a stop, as Korey pulled over and looked at me in disbelief.

"You're what?"

"I'm pregnant and it's Tre's baby."

"Oh my goodness…"

"I didn't mean for this to happen, Korey," I said bursting into tears.

"Are you ok?" she asked softly.

"Yes," I replied, trying to pull myself together.

We drove the rest of the way in complete silence. She pulled up to my door and said nothing. As I moved to get out, she grabbed my arm and said, "I won't say anything."

"Thank you," I replied gratefully, as I got out and closed the door.

Chapter 24

The knock on my door came much sooner than I'd expected. I knew he would come, just didn't think it would be that fast. At first, I just laid in the bed and slowly counted to one hundred, but then he started yelling.

"Bitch, I know you're in there! You better open this fucking door right now, Timberlynn!" he threatened.

The last thing I needed right now was for Wanda to come running over here to see what all the commotion was about, so I got up and opened the door. As soon as it opened, he pushed it in, grabbed me, pushed me down on the bed, and wrapped both his hands around my neck.

"You actually came to my house and jumped on my wife?" he asked menacingly without loosening his grip.

"Stop it...," I choked, "...I can't breathe..."

"You can't breathe, huh? Oh, I'm so sorry! Am I hurting you? What are you trying to do to me, huh?" he ranted, as he released my neck and began to shake me.

I tried to fight back but he was too strong. The next thing I knew, he had my arms pinned above my head with one hand and was slapping my face with the other. I tried to move my head to dodge his blows, but my movement was limited since he had me totally pinned down.

"Stop it! Please...the baby," I pleaded crying hysterically. All of a sudden, he crushed his lips down on mine and forced his tongue into my mouth. He released my hands and cupped my face and I grabbed the back of his head and held him to me. Before I could stop myself from responding, we were both naked and rolling around on the floor like animals.

After it was over, we both lay on the floor exhausted. I got up and threw on a T-shirt and sat on the bed starring out the window. I was so confused and conflicted. I didn't understand why he was doing this to me. One minute he wanted to be with his wife and the next he was screwing me. I didn't know if I was coming or going, but I did know that I didn't want him to leave me.

A few minutes later, he got up and put on his clothes. He turned and looked at me for a long time and then said, "Don't you ever come to my house again, Timberlynn, and I mean that. Don't talk to me at work either. We are through. If I catch you around my crib again, I am going to hurt you."

I couldn't believe what I was hearing! This man had just made love to me and now he was going to stand there and tell me to stay away from him? I was beside myself with rage. Before I could register what was happening, I heard an inhumane scream come from inside myself as I lunged at him. I tried to tear his eyes out but he held my arms away from his face, as he struggled to keep me from overpowering him.

"You bastard!" I screamed, as I continued to fight him. Suddenly, the door flew open and Wanda rushed in with a bat wielded and ready to strike. Tre looked startled, as he pushed me to the floor and jumped over the bed to put distance between himself and the bat.

"Get your hands off of her!" Wanda yelled. I just stayed on the floor and cried.

"You ok, Sugarpie?" she asked kneeling down to make sure I wasn't hurt. No words would come, all I could do was lie there and rock back and forth.

"That girl is crazy!" Tre shot back, as he made his way to the door. "You stay away from me and my wife or I will have you arrested."

"Get your sorry ass off my property before I have you arrested," Wanda shouted back, waving the bat in his direction.

He walked out slamming the door behind him and then Wanda turned her attention to me.

"Did he hurt you? Tell me…"

"I…I'm ok. Wanda, what am I going to do?" I wailed.

"Shhh…," she crooned, "it'll be alright. You just wait and see, ok? You'll see," she promised, as she rocked me back and forth.

My sobs subsided as I listened to Wanda's heartbeat while she rocked with me. As I swayed to and fro, my mind formulated a way to make all of my problems disappear and pay Tre back at the same time. It was so simple that I was mad at myself for not thinking of it a long time ago.

I decided that it was truly time for my days on this earth to end and this time I was not going to fail. The only difference in the approach would be that this time, I was going to have an audience for my final farewell. If he couldn't love me in life, I was going to make sure that he didn't forget me in death.

Chapter 25

"I'm sorry, Timberlynn, but I have to let you go," Mr. Griffin said sadly. "Tre has filed a restraining order against you and after reading the report, there is no way that I can continue to allow you to work here."

All I could do was sit there speechless. I couldn't believe that he had actually managed to get me fired! What was I going to do now? Who was going to hire a pregnant girl with no real work experience? I felt myself start to panic, as I fought desperately to keep my composure.

"Are you alright, Timberlynn?" Mr. Griffin asked, with a look of genuine concern on his face.

"Yes," I whispered hoarsely.

"I'm truly sorry that this had to happen."

"It's not your fault, Mr. Griffin. Thank you for giving me a chance," I said, as I got up and headed toward the door.

"Wait a minute," he said suddenly, as he hurried from his desk to join me at the door. He gave me a fatherly hug and said, "You take care of yourself, ok?"

I shook my head and hurried out before the tears began to fall. While I cleaned out my locker, Korey came in and sat on the bench and watched sadly as I gathered my things.

"Are you alright?" she asked.

"No," I choked as I burst into tears. "What am I going to do? I'm pregnant and now I don't have a job! That bastard! I can't believe he would do this to me!"

Korey jumped up and hugged me tight.

"You'll be alright," she said smiling, "You came down here a scared little girl from Grand Rapids and look at you now! You got a job, a place to stay, and you whoopin' ass and takin' names!"

I laughed and hugged her back.

"Thank you for all you've done for me."

"Don't mention it. Just do me a favor?"

"What?"

"Stay out of trouble and stay away from Tre," she said seriously.

I didn't respond, instead I smiled weakly, as I grabbed my things and walked out. Not really wanting to deal with lengthy good-byes and questions, I opted to go quietly out the back door.

After I boarded the bus and found a seat, I replayed all the events of the last few months in my mind. The clarity that I had in that ten-minute ride to the motel was mind-boggling. I was a complete idiot for allowing this man to ruin my life this way. True enough, I could have avoided it all, but all I ever wanted was for someone to love me. He saw that in me and used it to his advantage.

By the time I got to my room, I was seething! First he'd taken advantage of me, made me fall in love with him, knocked me up, threw me away like a dishrag, and now he'd made me lose my job! My mind was made up. I didn't have anything else to lose, so now it was time for him to see just how far he had pushed me.

My life was not going to go on like this for another day. First my family deserted me and now Tre. How could I bring a child into this world? I wasn't capable of inspiring love from my own parents, so how could I expect to love and raise a child?

"It wouldn't be fair, so I'll just end it all today," I told myself, as I took the gun out of my drawer and headed to my final destination.

Chapter 26

As I made my final trip, I wondered if I should have left Wanda a note or some kind of letter telling how much I loved her and appreciated her kindness to me. She was the only true friend I had ever had. I knew she was going to be heartbroken when she heard the news and I was sorry for that.

I had to walk six miles to get to Tre's house from the motel because I didn't want to take the bus, and risk getting caught with a gun in my purse. The way my luck had been, that's exactly what would've happened. I just wanted to get this over with, as soon as possible.

"What a sad and short life", I thought to myself, as I approached his driveway. I was nineteen years old and this day was to be my last. I thought about my mother and father and wondered what they would do when they heard the news. What about Skye? Would she cry? It comforted me to think that they loved me enough to cry a little. Oh well, couldn't dwell on that or I would never get this over with.

Tre's car was parked in the driveway, so I made my way to the back door. I stood in the backyard and peeked through the window, and saw that it was completely dark on the first floor. I backed up a little and saw that there were lights on upstairs, in what looked to be the bathroom. I could tell by the contact paper that was placed on the window to keep outsiders from looking in.

I knew from living with Tre, that he loved to take long showers. I really hoped that he was enjoying this one, because he was about to get the surprise of his life after he finished.

The back door was one that had four small stained glass windows that made up one big window. I took a brick from the flower landscaping and carefully broke a pane out of the back window. After cleaning the glass out, I reached through and unlocked the door.

Once inside, I stopped to make sure that there was no alarm and then proceeded on to the stairs. I could hear the water running in the shower, as I ascended the stairs and approached the bathroom, so I took a detour and went into their bedroom.

This bedroom was nothing like the room we'd shared at the apartment. Clearly Brooke's tastes reigned supreme in this house. Everything in the room was crème and purple. It was surprising to me that Tre could sleep in here without getting sick to his stomach, since everything about him was so masculine.

I opened her walk-in closet and gasped. She had enough clothes to cloth a family of five for a whole year. There were tons of named brand suits, designer jeans in every color, dresses with the tags still on them, and probably over fifty pairs of shoes. I came out of the closet and listened; the water was still running.

"That's my boy," I said to myself, "make sure you're nice and clean for me, baby."

I sat down casually on the bed and made myself comfortable. After settling into a favorable position, I felt a flutter in my stomach.

My hand immediately went to the spot where I'd just felt the tingling sensation. For an instant, I regretted what I was about to do to myself and to my innocent child. I began to second-guess my rash decision to end our lives without considering all of the options. But, just at the moment when I may have reconsidered, I heard the water go off in the bathroom and all the rage and hurt returned in an instant.

I reached into my purse and pulled out the gun. The metal felt extremely cold and heavy in my clammy hand. Flipping off the safety, I got comfortable again and waited. Before long, I heard the bathroom door open and footsteps coming down the hall. The pistol was cocked and readily aimed at my head, when the door opened.

It was Brooke who was in the shower, not Tre! She stood in the doorway with one hand holding her towel and the other one covering her mouth. Her eyes were the size of quarters, as she stared at me in disbelief.

"What are you doing?" she shrieked. "Don't do that! Please put that away!"

I sat there dumbfounded, with the gun pressed to my head, and my finger poised ready to pull the trigger. This is not the way it was supposed to happen! Tre's car was in the driveway, so he was supposed to be the one standing here right now!

"Timberlynn, please put the gun away," she pleaded, "we can get you some help, ok?"

"I don't need your help! I need to see Tre. Where is he?"

"He's not here," she replied still trying to remain calm.

"Shit!" I swore. Now everything was messed up! Then I heard the door slam downstairs.

"Brooke!" Tre yelled, as he made his way to the stairs.

When I heard his voice, I panicked and pointed the gun at Brooke. "Get over there in that chair! Now!" I ordered and she scurried to sit down at the vanity table near the wall.

"Brooke, why is there broken glass..." Tre stopped short when he walked into the room and saw the scene that was quickly unfolding before his eyes.

There I was, standing next to his precious wife holding a gun to her head. This was not what I had planned, not at all. I did not want to hurt anybody, just myself. She wasn't supposed to be there. I kept thinking to myself that I had to figure out something and fast.

"Timberlynn, what are you doing?" he asked slowly.

"I came here to show you what you have driven me to, Tre. I wanted you to see that you were responsible for my death and the death of your unborn child, but you weren't home and now we have a problem."

"Unborn child," Brooke gasped in disbelief.

"Yes, his unborn child. You didn't tell your wife that we were having a baby, Tre?" I asked laughing crazily.

"Brooke she's lying," he said.

"No, Brooke, I'm not lying! He took my virginity on my eighteenth birthday and got me pregnant during the time you were separated! Tell her!" I screamed.

"Baby..." he pleaded to her helplessly.

"Look at me!" I screamed, "You said you loved me!"

"Timberlynn, I swear if you hurt her... I'll..." he began.

"You'll what? You can't hurt me anymore, Tre."

Just then, Brooke turned and lunged towards me, and the next thing I heard was the sound of a single gunshot. It was as if time moved in slow motion after the sound. First I heard the shot, then I saw brain matter splatter all over the wall, and then her body fell lifelessly to the floor.

"Noooo..." Tre screamed, as he ran to help his dying wife.

The gun fell from my hand, and I began to scream. Even as they were putting the cuffs on my wrists, I screamed. I screamed for hours. I don't remember when I stopped, but I screamed until my throat wouldn't allow me to scream anymore.

Chapter 27

Timberlynn was lost in the memory of what happened that dreadful night. With her head buried in her arms, her body shook violently as she sobbed. I didn't know what to say as I tried to regain my own composure.

I was completely mortified by the story that I had just heard. That poor woman lost her life at the expense of a cheating husband, who had toyed with a young girl. Even though the gruesome outcome was hardly excusable on Timberlynn's part, my heart still went out to her. Maybe if her parents had shown her a little more love and attention, she never would have felt the desperate need to seek it from a married man.

I sat there silently and stared at the young girl, trying to figure out what to say next. She was consumed with grief over what she had done. No wonder she couldn't sleep at night and wanted my help in making everyone understand what happened!

"I'm so sorry! I didn't mean to hurt her…" she said between sobs, "I just wanted him to see…I never meant for it to happen. She moved and the gun went off…please forgive me…"

I was at a total loss! I didn't have the power to forgive anyone.

"I can't sleep at night! I see things when I'm awake! I can't live like this anymore, so you have to make them understand that I didn't mean it! I didn't mean to hurt Brooke, it was an accident!"

By this time, she was exhausted and emotionally spent. We didn't have much time left and I still had to finish the interview.

"Timber," I began tentatively, "what happened to your baby?"

She looked up at me with unmasked pain in her eyes and said, "I'll never forget it…"

Chapter 28

By the time I was sentenced, I was seven months pregnant. My charge was manslaughter and I was sentenced to fifteen years of hard time, which I was ordered to begin serving immediately.

Wanda was in court everyday showing me her love and support. She cried harder than I did when I received my sentence. Mine were tears of regret that they didn't sentence me to die. I looked sadly at Wanda as they led me away. I desperately wanted to hug her and tell her that everything would be alright, but I couldn't.

After my first month in prison, I received my first visitors- my parents. There sat my mother and father looking just the same as I remembered. My mother's eyes were red and swollen from crying and my father's face was set, his eyes unreadable.

I said nothing as I sat down, picked up the phone, and waited for them to speak.

My mother spoke first. "Hello, Timberlynn," she said.

I said nothing.

"Are you holding up ok in here?" she asked.

"I guess," I responded dryly.

My mother broke down and gave the phone to my father. He held the receiver to his ear for a long moment and then said, "So what is going to happen to the baby?"

"I don't know."

"Timberlynn, how could this happen? Why did you do this to us? First, you run away like a thief in the night, we don't hear from you in over two years, and now this? We thought you were dead and now you turn up in jail for murder?!" he said heatedly.

At that moment, any love that I'd ever felt for my parents disappeared. The whole time my father was speaking, I sat there with the phone to my ear and watched his lips move. These were the same people that made me feel like I was less than nothing my entire life.

They didn't come with loving words to tell me that they would always love me no matter what. They didn't apologize for the way they'd always acted like I didn't exist except when there was a problem. They didn't promise that they would do whatever they could to help me. They didn't ask to hear my side of the story. Instead, my mother sat and cried tears of self-pity and my father blamed me for their embarrassment. At that moment, I realized that I hated them with every fiber of my being. The feeling overwhelmed me to the point that I began to tremble.

"Are you done?" I asked my father. He was so taken aback by the callous tone in my voice that he said nothing.

"Why did you come here? Was it to ease your mind and tell yourselves that you did all you could to save me? Is that it, mom? What the fuck are you crying for? I'm the one that has to live out the rest of my days in this place. Does my language shock you, mother? I have to tell you, I learned a lot living on my own…" I paused for effect and to allow the weight of my words to sink in.

"I learned that the world is a cold hard place when nobody loves you. I also learned that a woman looking to find love in the wrong places can be very dangerous. Did I mean for this to happen? Hell no! I was going to kill myself! I didn't mean to hurt anyone!"

"Maybe if you pieces of shit would've treated me like a daughter, then maybe I wouldn't have had to leave home to try to find it elsewhere! Please allow me to ease your minds…I take full responsibility for what I did. Now you can leave here with a clear conscience. Just go and forget that I exist because I don't ever want to see either of you again," I spat and slammed the phone down. The look on my father's face gave me all the satisfaction I needed, while my mother just sat there and cried harder.

The guard came in to take me back to my cell and as I was led out of the room, I didn't look back.

Late one night, two months later, I went into labor in my cell and was rushed to the infirmary. After nine hours of excruciating pain, my baby girl was born. The nurse that delivered her was very kind to me. She allowed me to hold my baby after she'd cleaned her up even though she knew she wasn't supposed to.

She was beautiful. I looked at her and counted her fingers and toes to make sure that they were all there. She looked just like me with her dark hair and smooth caramel complexion, but she had Tre's eyes.

It was amazing to me how something that caused so much pain could be so perfect. I couldn't believe that I'd almost ended her life before it had even begun. Never had I felt as much love in my heart, as I did when I held my baby for the first time.

Just as I leaned over to kiss her cheek, one of the head nurses came in and scolded the kind nurse for breaking the rules. She then snatched her right out of my arms. I tried to hold on to her but she started to cry. The sound of my baby's cries hurt my heart…so I let her go. I let her go and I never saw her again. They took my baby out of my arms and I never saw her again.

After that, it just seemed like my life was worthless. I couldn't sleep at night because of the vivid nightmares and when I was awake, all I could do was cry for my baby. I had no idea what they did with her and it was making me crazy. I couldn't eat or sleep and the lack of food and rest was starting to make me hallucinate…I think.

I began to imagine that Brooke was following me around with an accusing look on her face and the side of her head blown out. She would just come out of nowhere and it would send me into hysterics. The other inmates avoided me because they thought I was crazy. I didn't blame them…I thought I was crazy too…

Chapter 29

"...and that's why I had to talk to you, Ms. Jackson," she cried desperately, "I had to tell my story and make everyone understand that I didn't mean it. I had to tell it so I can sleep at night and make her go away. Can you do that? Huh? Can you please?"

I couldn't do anything but sit there and stare at her with unmasked pity in my eyes. She was so young and so tormented and the circumstances were truly heartbreaking. I wanted to comfort her but I knew from past experience that it was not allowed, so I sat and watched silently as her little frame shook from her sobs of anguish.

Finally, after a long moment she looked up at me through her tears and said, "Do you think that God will forgive me?"

The question caught me completely off guard. I had no idea how to answer, so I just shook my head and said, "I believe that God will forgive anything if you ask Him."

"Don't worry, Ms. Jackson..." she said, "I won't kill myself like that other lady did. I don't deserve it. I will be strong and I will serve my time. I would just like for everyone, including Tre, to know that I never meant to hurt anyone...but myself."

From the corner of my eye I saw the guard moving in to undo her restraints to take her back to her cell so I replied quickly, "Don't you worry, Timber, I will make sure that everyone knows what happened…I promise."

"Thank you," she whispered gratefully.

I smiled weakly as they led her out of the room and watched the door slam behind them.

"Why do I keep doing this to myself?" I thought out loud.

Driving down the street moments later, I thought back on the story that I'd just heard. I wasn't sure what part of her tale perplexed me the most.

Was it the fact that there were actually men in this world that were heartless enough to toy with a woman's heart in the manner that Tre did to Timberlynn, or the fact that there were women in the world who were really weak enough to allow that to happen? Granted, the poor girl was clearly neglected by her parents, but if she was strong enough to leave that life behind and prosper, then why wasn't she strong enough to walk away from a relationship that was obviously unhealthy?

Those unanswered questions still plagued my mind, as I stared at the blank computer screen in front of me. The office was empty except for the cleaning lady, Myra, who was emptying my garbage can.

"Myra, why do you think that women stay with men that cheat?" I asked.

"I don't know Miss Jackson…could be that nowadays it's hard to find a man and a good man is damn near impossible. I suppose that some of us are so desperate for love that we just settle for the first thing that comes along," she replied thoughtfully.

"Yeah," I said more to myself than to her. After sitting in deep thought for a while longer, I began to type the story that I hoped would help the world understand why a young girl would murder her lover's wife.

Chapter 30

"You know what, Vanessa," Yolanda, the Woman's Lib editor began, as she threw a copy of the latest issue on my desk, "I really think that you've hit a goldmine with this prison angle! I mean the public has been eating this stuff up, first the Marion Hayes story and now this. Just think…I had to twist your arm to get you to do it in the first place!"

I smiled to myself, as I listened to her ramble on about how she was right and I was wrong. The story was a huge success. The office had received a ton of letters expressing sympathy and pleas to the justice system on Timberlynn's behalf. I gathered all of the letters and sent them to her to keep.

I sincerely hoped that reading the public's reaction to her story would give her some kind of peace of mind. My mind could not fathom what it would be like to have to live with the murder of an innocent human being on my conscience, day after day.

My happiness over the success of my article was short lived, when I received a call from the front desk informing me that Tre Stevens was waiting to see me. I couldn't imagine what would bring that man to my office of all places, but I told her to send him back.

When he walked through my door, I immediately understood why Timberlynn had found him so appealing. He was fine, no doubt about that.

His clothes hugged him in all the right places allowing his muscular physique to show, and he had an air of cockiness about him, that I was sure that most women found irresistible.

"Hello, Mr. Stevens. What can I do for you?" I asked politely, as I motioned for him to have a seat in front of my desk.

"Well for starters, you can stop writing stories that make criminals look like the victims," he snapped.

Suddenly, the reason for his visit became crystal clear. He was upset because I had made him look bad and he was probably catching all kinds of flack about it.

"Well, Mr. Stevens, I'm sorry if the story I did offended you in anyway but that is the story that was told by Ms. Crawford and that is what I was hired to do…tell her story," I replied.

"Yeah? Tell her story? Well what about my dead wife's story? Some crazy bitch breaks into our house, shoots my wife in the head, and she is the one that should be pitied? I'm the bad guy? Does that sound right to you?"

By this time, I was beginning to get more than a little fed up with his self- righteous attitude. I silently counted to ten and then chose my words carefully before I responded.

"In no way did I try to justify what Timberlynn did or lessen the loss that you have suffered, Mr. Stevens," I said evenly, "The purpose of the stories that the Women's Lib has been doing on these female inmates, is to try to help people understand why these women would commit such heinous crimes."

"You need to be trying to write stories to help people figure out how to give those women what they deserve! An eye for an eye, not a chance to whine and cry in some fuckin' magazine! My wife was killed, dammit! Don't you care about that?" he yelled.

I could feel my sense of control starting to leave me, so I picked up my stress balls and began to twirl them in my hand. Once I felt that I could speak and maintain my composure I replied, "Of course I care about the fact that you lost your wife, Mr. Stevens…"

"No," he interjected, cutting me off, "all you care about is making a deadline and getting a story!"

At that point I lost it. "It seems to me, Mr. Stevens, that if you would have honored your marriage vows in the first place and not taken advantage of a young girl that you were clearly manipulating, then maybe, just maybe, it never would have happened! Yes, I feel sorry for your wife, because she should not have had to be involved in a bad situation that you created. But, since you couldn't keep your dick in your pants, a lot of lives have been ruined! So don't you come in here with your self-righteous attitude and try to tell me that I'm wrong for telling the truth!"

He looked at me as if I had slapped him in the face. Tre Stevens didn't say another word as he got up and stormed out of my office. I fell back into my chair and let out a deep breath. I couldn't believe that I had gone off on him like that. My co-workers huddled around my door to find out what all of the commotion was about.

"I'm ok," I told them, "just another satisfied customer."

Epilogue

Timberlynn Crawford's story was laid to rest, and I never saw or heard from Tre Stevens again. I did receive a phone call from Wanda and I found that to be very comforting.

On the day that she called I was researching my next project, when my phone rang.

"Hello," I answered.

"Hello, Ms. Jackson, this is Wanda… Timber's friend."

"What a pleasure it is to hear from you, Wanda! What can I do for you?"

"Well…" she began, "I just wanted to thank you for what you did for my little Sugarpie. She's a good girl and it really hurt me to think that everyone would believe that she was some crazed murderer or something. Thanks to you, now everyone knows the truth and now they can judge fairly on they own. You know?"

"Yes, I know," I said smiling.

"Well…I don't want to take up too much of your time, just wanted to thank you."

"And thank you for calling."

With that in the can, it was on to my next assignment; Dawn Langston. This was a woman who was sentenced to two life sentences, for torturing and killing her sister's accused murderer.

My findings in this case left very little hope that I would be able to find any level of understanding from this woman. The photos taken of the body of the man she'd killed were extremely gruesome, and lead me to believe that this woman had to be crazy and demented to do the things that were done to this man. Murderer or otherwise.

It seemed like the further along I went with this project, the more violent the crimes became. I had to brace myself for this one, because I had a feeling that it was going to be one hell of a story to tell.

Look for these other books by Janaya Black

The Prison Chronicles-
The Breaking Point
As Told By the Other Woman

Also visit www.black-smithenterprises.com or www.myspace.com/thebreakingpointmovie to get more information on upcoming projects.

Wayne Whitfield
Home 623-0150
cell 244-4012
61 Manson Pl